AN IMPRINT OF

# SCHOOL OF

D1531991

"A hugely impressive first nove... ...music, friendship and obsession. Gripping and emotional"     DAVID NICHOLLS

"Rubin writes with grace and exactitude, giving a tangible, animated quality to the sensual world of his story... this is a luminous, quiet storm of a novel that resounds long after its heartbreaking coda"     *GUARDIAN*

"An elegant, synaesthetic tale... Gatsby-like"     *FT*

"Overtones of Patricia Highsmith... the world of talented youth is a captivating backdrop... a very pleasant interlude"

*IRISH TIMES*

"I adored this debut. It's a fascinating dissection of the power of friendship"     *IRISH EXAMINER*

"The writing is poised and lyrical, with all the rhythm and some of the ache of the Faurés and Debussys it dwells upon. Echoes of Gatsby are subtly embedded... a writer to watch"

*BIG ISSUE*

"A beautifully written debut novel about obsession and repression"     *ATTITUDE*

"It's about huge and basic emotions: insecurity, friendship, need, sex. It delivers all of this in elegantly readable prose, efficient yet deeply moving. I loved it"     *ELLE THINKS*

# ERIC BECK RUBIN

# SCHOOL
## *of*
# VELOCITY

AN IMPRINT OF PUSHKIN PRESS

ONE
an imprint of Pushkin Press
71–75 Shelton Street, London WC2H 9JQ

Published in Canada by Doubleday Canada, a division of
Penguin Random House Canada Limited in 2016

First published in Great Britain by ONE in 2016
This edition first published by ONE in 2017

1 3 5 7 9 8 6 4 2

ISBN 978 0 993506 29 1

Text designed and set in Scala by Tetragon, London
Printed and bound by CPI Group (UK) Ltd, Croydon CRO 4YY

www.pushkinpress.com

# SCHOOL
*of*
# VELOCITY

I t's my third time performing in Aachen. The previous two were all-Ravel programs. This time I've been booked in, last minute, to accompany a cellist for Fauré's "Elegy."

I had almost turned the offer down. It's been six months since I've practised in any kind of productive way and over a year since I've taken the stage with confidence.

But I was told the cellist I'd be accompanying was young and American and that was the hook. The fact she's young connected it to my own first overseas tour, at the centre of all my recent thoughts; the fact she's American snared me with a different nostalgia, just as powerful.

You've been waiting for this, I told myself. An actual examination of my condition. A performance where the results would be clearer than any lab test or thought experiment. This concert, because it was last minute, something I couldn't cheat, was the way to decide, ultimately, whether I could go forward or needed to go back.

Though I know the Fauré by heart, and have performed it dozens of times, I'd still normally spend the run-up practising the piece, smoothing the edges and trying to develop something new in my interpretation. But as this is out of the question, I instead spend the remaining days in pent-up anticipation. Mostly I picture myself waiting in the wings, peering past the curtain. I watch as the audience files down the aisles and shuffles across the rows. Look up at the acoustic reflectors and other objects hanging from the ceiling. Then, in my mind's eye, the house lights start to blink. The ushers put away their programs and begin to close the doors. I look out to the stage. The Bösendorfer 280 VC. A resting beast about to be poked awake.

Sometimes I let myself wander farther and walk onstage. I feel the boards creak underfoot. The faint breeze of air conditioning on the back of my neck. But as I get closer to the piano things start to go wrong. Disruptions. Insensitivity. Oversensitivity. The piece I know backwards and forwards, diminishing till I can't hear it, then growing so loud it threatens to burst through my head. What's next? A needling, high-pitched ringing? A cascade of notes, raining down like hammers from the ceiling of the concert hall? In my imagination I can't separate what I fear from what I secretly want.

Normally I meet the soloist the day before a performance to rehearse. She'll explain her general approach to the piece, make specific instructions, and we'll play through several times. She'll lead and I'll take notes. How slow will we be with the opening? How robust with the sharps in the third line? How dramatic the swings from pianissimo to fortissimo through the middle section?

But as everything in Aachen is last minute, including the cellist's scheduled arrival, there's no time set aside. She and I meet in the green room, one hour before the show, for a quick introduction and to exchange ideas and references, then she slips off to her dressing room.

And I go back to mine, with half an hour till call, to wait.

I flip through the score. Examine and re-examine myself in the mirror. Test that the doorknob still works, and I'm not trapped inside. When I run out of distractions I look at the clock on the wall, ten minutes left, and that's when I start to hear it. It comes in a rush. A violent, disorganized throb of noise. Pouring into my ears, bluring the edges of my vision.

A knock on the door.

"Time, Mister de Vries."

Dread and giddiness run through me as I move through the halls backstage. Is it too late to stop? I ask. But isn't the point to go through with it, no matter what? I get to the wings and see the cellist, technical crew, stage manager. Focused on their own tasks. Not one of them has a clue what I'm hearing right now. Notes from the opening bars of the Fauré, some kind of a steam engine whistle, and, overriding it all, clashes of sounds that have nothing to do with the music, or any music. Boiling inside my head.

I step away from the group to a spot just beside the curtain and look out to the concert hall. The audience is filing in. The ushers are standing by the doors. I peer out to the back row, left, and start scanning. I try to look at the face of each person in his or her seat, turning program pages, unwrapping candies, speaking to the person in the next seat. It's my pre-concert routine. Meant to anaesthetize. But as I move down the rows, I can't shake the thought of the mistakes I've made these past few years. Quintets where I've confused one player with another. Accompaniments where I've lost track of the soloist. Concerts where I've come in late and thrown off the timing. Not that anyone would tell me, of course. No, the other musicians would just shake my hand afterwards, say something about catching a train or flight, and walk out the back door, leaving me guessing what I'd done wrong because I couldn't have known for sure.

As I scan the faces in the rows I wait for the music of the opening bars to step forward from the noise inside my head. If I can just pick out that starting passage, a clean first bar, I might be able to walk onstage and let my fingers and hands and the rest of my body take over.

The house lights start blinking, hurrying the last ticket holders to their seats. I stop scanning the rows. I step back from the curtain and accidentally brush against the cellist.

"I'm sorry," she says. Or at least, that's what I think she says. I mutter a few words and turn away. Where are those first notes? I close my eyes and try to organize the noise, like a conductor marshalling an orchestra, but it isn't working. It's getting worse. Hammering, metallic tearing, a buzz saw swinging left to right. I fix my posture, try to regain focus by looking at the Bösendorfer ten feet away, but the stage lights flash on and the phosphorescent white reflecting off the keys makes it too bright to look at.

Applause begins to swell. I can hear it. The stage manager gestures, and the soloist, grasping her cello by the neck, marches onstage. I follow at a distance, to the piano, and sink into the bench. I feel for the knobs to adjust the height but my shaking wrists can hardly make them work. The cellist brushes her hair behind her bare shoulder and angles her chair towards the open lid of the piano. She positions her fingers above the cello's strings and inhales.

Now is the moment. I *have* to hear the clean opening of the Fauré. But as an especially cruel joke all I can make out is music from a completely different piece, a different genre. I sit completely still, waiting to place my fingers above the keys, waiting to begin, but the noise keeps coming. More notes, more sound. Every triad, chord, arpeggio, but none that makes any sense.

I look to the soloist, try to tell her I'm not ready, but she mistakes my glance for the beginning of a silent count. I shake my head to tell her to stop, but the side-to-side movement sends blows through my skull. A terrible shrieking, an overriding throng of noise. Everything pressing to the front.

I force the bench back—I have to stop her—and try to stand.

The last thing I see is a stagehand rushing to me, mouthing words. I look up at the burning white stage lights, then see a veil of black dropping in front of my eyes. Somewhere, in the last alert part of my mind, I tell myself I've passed the test. Passed or failed, depending. But it's all the same. The choice is made. And though I'm suffering as badly as I ever have, a small part of me dances in a kind of ecstasy.

Two days later. The apartment in Maastricht. Alone, because Lena is up north for the month, with her mother.

I take a walk early in the day, while the sky is bright. "Extreme clear," as the pilots say, and I have to shade my eyes as I cross the river. For the first time in ages, I wait at corners for lights to change. I look both ways before stepping onto the street. I take my time on the steep cobbled alleys around the old city. I know I'm overdoing it, but I don't want some hidden part of me to sabotage this. Not after I've come so far and am so close.

The noise during the walk is like the cries of seagulls circling in the air. Now and then I catch traces of the Fauré.

Back at the apartment, I go to the piano, the walnut Bechstein baby grand, pull the tuning equipment from inside the bench, and lay it on the floor. I unfasten the piano's lid and delicately lean it against the wall. For the next three hours I stand over the soundboard and pick at the hammers, strings, and bridges, using mutes and levers and an electronic tuner. I test every note, left to right, and when I'm done I go through all eighty-eight in the opposite direction. The electronic tuner flashes a green light when I've got the balance right. You win: a perfectly tuned, concert ready, Model A.

I use one of the rags from under the kitchen sink to clean discolourations from the keys and fingerprint smudges along the fall. Try to lift the circles left by tall glasses and teacups on either side of the stand. When the case is shiny again, I do a quick once-over on the mother-of-pearl inlay on the body, then firmly refasten the lid drop and lid to the top of the piano.

It looks sharp. As good as the day I first saw it. As Lena and I first saw it.

It would be another two weeks before she got back. By then, I'd be settled elsewhere. I'd be able to explain.

I look out the window and see the sun beginning to set over the river. Soon it will sink into the horizon, make the river disappear, and cover the old town of Maastricht in shadow.

I skirt the piano and open the practice room closet. The old shoebox full of letters and other correspondence is on the top shelf. The paraphernalia, personal and professional, is in a cove at the back. My black leather overnight bag, the one that comes with me on tour, hangs from a hook. The idea is to pack everything in the bag. I try. The bag is fit to burst and the zipper won't close, but I don't mind.

In the bedroom I lay out socks, underwear, undershirt, a collarless white dress shirt in dry cleaner's plastic, and a tan garment bag I've dug out from the farther reaches of my closet. I unzip the bag halfway and look at the crisp midnight blue of the Nehru-style jacket with its covered buttons. My first suit, bought all those decades ago at the Hankyu Department Store, in Osaka.

I sit on my side of the bed and start undressing. I fold my underclothes, slip them in the proper drawers, and fall back onto the mattress.

It always gets worse as the day goes on, and now, just before sleep, is when I'm most susceptible. Dizziness, nausea, weakness, clashing noises trying to confuse me. I force my thoughts into order. Start from the top, I tell myself, like the imaginary conductor in front of his orchestra. First movement, how this story started. Second, where it went wrong. Third, what came after. Lena. My condition. The doctors and their diagnoses.

On this night, I let the sounds play all they want. Tomorrow morning I'll be in my car, suited and booted, driving up the A2. Heading to where the farmers' fields give way to swaths of grass. To where the trees line the sides of the highway like an honour guard. To the Gestelseweg exit, where I'll turn off and look for the lights, where I'll take the right and follow the narrow street to the end. Where it's been waiting all these thirty years.

Home.

# PRACTICE

I saw Dirk before I met him. I saw him several times before I even knew his name. He was like a new word that, once learned, you heard spoken everywhere. Compelling attention. Mine, yours, anyone's.

The first time Dirk directly crossed my path, though, was at an after-school music rehearsal. I was in line next to the temporary stage at the back of the room, looking over the crowd, waiting for my girlfriend, Lise. We were both in grade nine, new in town, and new to the school, Sint Ansfried, where Lise was in the drama program and I was in the music program.

Sint Ansfried was the first arts school I attended, but I had been in music classes since I was a child. It was my parents' idea at first, but something that became my identity. Other children played sports and games and went to camp over the summer. I was at the keyboard, spending hours on my own every day. My parents were proud. Their son was quiet. Diligent. It took the buzzing halls of Sint Ansfried to see this could also be loneliness. That I had met Lise and asked her out, even if she'd gotten one of her friends to tell me to, was a miracle. We'd been going out for close to four weeks.

"Vollweg! Fortuyn!"

Two of the students in front of me. I looked over to the door again and that's when Lise walked in. She was with her friend Stefa, also in the drama program, and someone else I recognized. A stormcloud of dark wavy hair, school sweater tied around his waist, shirttails out, and sleeves rolled above his elbows. His locker was near mine and I had seen him loping through the halls, calling out people's names and crashing the lunchtime card games. He liked to throw in expressions from other languages when he spoke. *Hola. Basta.* And here he was, with Lise. Mister Everywhere, Señor Todas-Partes.

"Zapirli! Baumwolle!"

I'd be up next. I had two pieces for rehearsal that day. Chopin's étude no. 3 in E Major, called the "Tristesse," and the *Gnossiennes* by Erik Satie, a slow and eerie walk through the woods. I looked down at the notes I had written on the sheet music, trying to ignore the tingling of excitement in my fingers. I was getting better at performing, but I preferred practising. No crowd to please. When I looked up I saw Lise and Stefa had found a seat at the back of the room on either side of Mister Everywhere. His arms were spread wide, his fingers dancing through the air. Lise and Stefa were leaning in. Soon he was also leaning in, covering his mouth to share a secret, his left hand resting on Stefa's shoulder.

"De Vries!"

As I walked up to the stage, I started playing the first bars of the étude in my head, establishing the pace with my imaginary left hand. Sitting on the bench, I put the sheet music on the stand, spread my fingers above the keyboard, and was about to start when, despite myself, I glanced across the room.

Was it possible that guy's hand was on Lise's shoulder, not Stefa's?

Focus, I said to myself, and began to play.

Later in the week, at the bike racks where we met most days after school, Lise told me Dirk was in her drama class. He'd been a child actor, she said, in a popular television show. "He played the younger brother. I must have watched him every day."

I knew the show. Was that why Dirk was familiar?

"The cast won a Goldie one year," Lise said, "and Dirk went onstage to accept it. It was against the rules but he said it was amazing."

We got on our bikes and cycled to Cromvoirt, where Lise lived. When we got to her house, we disembarked and went to the backyard, to the shed. The hinges of the shed door always moaned. Inside was bare except for an old couch, where Lise and I kissed. She lay on top, a small gold chain dangling in front of the curves of her breasts, tantalizing me.

That day, after Lise got up from the couch and tucked the chain beneath her shirt, she mentioned Dirk again. He did radio plays for the RNW, she said, and speaks English fluently. "He doesn't even have an accent."

❖

As I cycled from Cromvoirt to my house in Vlijmen, along the empty road and under an open sky, my thoughts kept turning to Dirk. The child actor who was on television and in radio plays and spoke English without an accent. That last bit, about having no accent. Was that really possible? Wouldn't he have *some* kind of accent?

That night I brought my dinner to the Grotrian upright in the living room, where my father was sitting on the couch, dictating charts. I wanted to work on the "Tristesse," specifically the second section. After a series of octaves, the left hand rumbles and the right hand is meant to soothe the pent-up harmonies in a string of notes that leads back to the opening melody. Recently, instead of leading to the opening melody, my right hand, going its own way, was drawing me back to the climbing and descending octaves. It was strange for me to make mistakes, and I'd made this one at the after-school rehearsal.

As I began my warm-ups, my mind wandered to the drama studio, the rehearsal. Had Dirk's hand really been on *Lise*'s shoulder? I remembered the glint of silver off his ring. I thought I saw it beside Lise's dark hair. Surely Dirk knew Lise had a boyfriend, even if he didn't know my name.

My father started speaking into the Dictaphone. "Patient Schutte, a lovely thirty-nine-year-old female, presented with mild—"

"I'm trying to practise, Dad."

My father switched off the Dictaphone and looked at me.

I looked back at my fingers, suspended a half-inch above the keys. I realized the mistake. I'd been using the third instead of the fourth finger for a particular triad and it was shifting me from major to minor. I took a pencil from next to the stand and wrote "4" above the vexing note, indicating finger usage.

I restarted the section slowly, right hand only. With each correct run-through, I sped up, and eventually added the left hand.

My father folded up his charts and took my dinner plate to the kitchen. I repeated the section a few more times. Dirk must have known Lise had a boyfriend. Which meant he knew about me. Knew I existed, if nothing more.

"Paging Old Man Johannes de Vriesland!"

It was within a week of the rehearsal that I first heard Dirk call out my name, or his version of it. I was at my locker, between classes, and when I turned I saw him walking towards me, shirttails out, sleeves rolled up, feet splayed as he walked, tucking stray hairs behind his ear. When he stuck out his hand, I noticed the thick silver ring around his index finger.

"I was watching you the other day," he said, wiggling his fingers in the air. "Not bad."

When he smiled I saw one of his front teeth was chipped.

"So, I have the Budapest Radio Orchestra paying a visit to my living room after school today," he said, "and apparently they're short a piano soloist. Interested?"

That's how he invited me to his house. And it wasn't just me he invited. It was Lise too. And another girl, Beate, who was in the circle of lunchtime card players that Dirk sometimes nudged himself into. She was thin and tall with a crown of ginger curls.

At the last bell we met at the bicycle rack and left in pairs. Beate rode with Lise, I rode with Dirk, all of us heading towards the Sint Jan steeple, which marked the centre of Den Bosch. Dirk didn't introduce Beate as his girlfriend, he didn't introduce her at all, but when he and I put some distance between us and the girls, he leaned over, looked at me, and said he had seen Beate naked when the two of them had gone skinny-dipping in a neighbour's swimming pool. Before I could think of anything to say, or ask, Dirk's eyes were back on the road.

That afternoon was my first time in Den Bosch without my parents. Vlijmen, where we lived, was a postwar village, and Den Bosch was the nearest big city, where we sometimes visited on weekends. The roads near Dirk's house were cobblestone. The houses were tall, narrow, and close to the street. Where main-floor curtains were open you could see into living rooms. Chandeliers, oil paintings, old and ornate furniture, porcelain plates on display, and vases filled with flower arrangements. One after another, all alike.

At the end of a dead-end street Dirk pointed to an alley behind his house where Lise and I could lock our bikes, while he and Beate leaned theirs against a tree in the middle of a small fenced-in garden.

I expected Dirk's house to be like the ones I'd spied into on the way over, but it wasn't. The entranceway was tile, not hardwood. There was hardwood in the living room, but the furniture in it was simple and looked comfortable. The kitchen had a rectangular island at the centre and a small circular table by the bay window. I'd never been in a house that looked as inviting, or felt so immediately welcoming.

Dirk impatiently waved us upstairs. "I'll be there in a sec," he said. "Beate'll lead the way."

We walked through the living room and up the staircase. At the top was a narrow carpeted hall and the first door on the left was Dirk's room. It was about the same size as mine but completely crammed. A bunk bed, with the bottom bunk covered in baggy pillows and duvets. Rickety bookshelves overflowing with books, magazines, stacks of photographs, records, and, as a centrepiece, a hi-fi stereo system with silver turntable and shoebox-sized speakers. His desk was buried under papers, and his cupboard over-stuffed with shirts and sweaters and jeans, none of which was part of the school uniform. The walls were painted a deep blue-green and plastered with posters of bands I knew, like the Beatles and Ike and Tina Turner, and movies I'd never heard of, like *Dr. Strangelove* and *Amarcord*.

Dirk appeared, balancing a box of biscuits, bottle of milk, and four glasses. "Huzzah," he said. "Make yourselves at home. I mean, at my home."

Beate curled up on the bottom bunk, among the pillows. I settled against the bedpost. Lise asked for the bathroom.

Dirk directed her next door and plonked himself in the middle of the bottom bunk, scattering some of the biscuits.

As soon as the bathroom door closed, Dirk leaned towards me.

"So, Old Man de Vries," he said, "what's she like?"

"Lise?" I asked.

He laughed. "Yes, de Vries. Lise."

I didn't know what to say, or what he wanted to hear. Beate giggled.

Dirk cupped his hands in front of his chest and squeezed. "Have you . . . ?"

I shook my head.

He pursed his lips and nodded in a kind of sympathy. "Suction?" He opened his mouth and pointed to the tip of his wiggling tongue.

I was about to make up a lie when Lise appeared at the door.

"What did I miss?" she asked.

"We were just talking about eating soap," Dirk said, leaning back against the wall and yawning. "Your parents ever make you eat soap, de Vries? No? My parents sometimes do. Usually the translucent kind, which I prefer anyway."

Beate broke out into a full-blown laugh. Dirk shifted closer to me to make room for Lise, and in the same movement dangled his hand off my shoulder.

"So, de Vries, you just moved here, right?"

I nodded, conscious of his arm hanging there, wondering what it might be up to.

"Where were you before?" he asked.

"Haarlem," I said.

"School?"

"I went to an all-boys school," I said.

"I did too!" Dirk said. "Grades six and seven. Good times."

He told the story of the time he helped organize an overnight raid of a nearby girls' dormitory. He told the story of how every day before first bell a card circulated his homeroom that had a picture of a naked woman on it, and that everyone called her Bushwoman. He shared the rumour that the regular photography teacher at Sint Ansfried hadn't come back this year because he had been sleeping with a grade twelve student and that apparently someone had found *proof* in the school's darkroom.

When Dirk spoke seriously he bobbed his head and sometimes closed his eyes. When he got close to a punchline his sides began to shake in anticipation. All through the afternoon he left his arm hanging over my shoulder.

Was any one of Dirk's stories true? Did it matter? Lise and Beate were fixed to every word he said. And so was I.

When he was done, Dirk led us to the front door, leaving Beate in his room upstairs. He said he had to do homework, winking as he said the word, then observing almost philosophically that if he actually *did* his homework he wouldn't be failing half his classes.

While I went to the alley to unlock the bicycles, Dirk stayed in the glass vestibule outside the front door with

Lise. When I came back, his hand was on the back of her neck, and he was smiling while whispering in her ear. When he saw me he let go of Lise and, with the same hand, pointed to me.

"Janos Miklos sends his regrets about the Budapest Radio Orchestra and says we'll do it next time, okay?"

Lise and I rode our bikes through the narrow streets and between the tall houses of Den Bosch and for the first time I cycled slightly ahead of Lise, pushing the pace. By the time we arrived in low-lying Cromvoirt, with its asphalt roads and bungalows, the sun was approaching the horizon and there was only a thin line of orange behind the silhouettes of far-off trees. Night coming, but still time. I was thinking of the gold chain hanging in front of Lise's breasts, and of Dirk cupping his hands in front of his chest. But as I was about to let my bike drop on the lawn in front of her house, Lise waved at me to stop.

"I have a scene to memorize for tomorrow," she said. "So not today."

The next Monday, I was sitting by the bike racks at the side entrance to Sint Ansfried. The last bell of the day had rung fifteen minutes before. Lise still hadn't come out.

Wind was rustling the branches. The sky was a light blue and criss-crossed by the double-lined vapour trails of passing airplanes. I replayed parts of the Chopin in my head to keep myself busy while I watched other students pour out the side door. First large groups, then stragglers.

When I saw there were fewer than a couple dozen bikes left in the rack I started to look for Lise's. It was my third time circling the rack, looking for the cream-coloured Batavus, when it dawned on me she was already gone.

I cycled as quickly as I could to Cromvoirt. Skidded left at the post office and right at the stop sign. I slid to a halt in the middle of the street in front of her house. Lise's Batavus lay on the lawn. Beside it was a bike I recognized.

I lay my bike on the curb, handles on the grass, and walked up to the back gate, where I peeked over the wooden slats. Still and barely breathing, I fixed my eyes on the little shed in the corner of the yard.

Of course I couldn't see any of it, but it was easy to imagine. Lise would have lain on the couch first, making room for Dirk beside her. After a moment he'd take her in his arms, kiss her with his tongue, and she'd kiss him with hers. Then Dirk would slide a hand to her waist and, when he sensed she was ready, slip it beneath her shirt, touch her bra. He had shown me exactly what he would do, and more or less told me he was going to do it, on the day he had invited me to his house.

I t's strange to say that's how it started for Dirk and me because that should have been how it ended.

I watched for two weeks as Dirk draped his hand over Lise's shoulder, fingertips fidgeting, thumb playing with ring. As he held her by the waist when they walked down the hall. As he laughed while she whispered into his ear. As he'd nod at her, or fix her hair.

Then it all changed. Lise started arriving at classes with Stefa, not Dirk. Walking the halls with eyes cast down and notebooks pressed to her chest. Hurrying away after the last bell without saying goodbye to anyone.

Dirk acted as if nothing had changed. He went on loping through the halls, loudly failing to blow bubble-gum bubbles, kicking the push-bars on the doors before proceeding through them. He returned to his group of friends, Pym, Pirm, and Beate, who was back in the picture, and dozens of others who naturally gravitated towards him.

Coincidentally, or so it seemed at the time, I began to see even more of Dirk. At the start of the school day while locking up my bike. Between classes while walking through the halls. During lunch hour in the cafeteria at the next table over. Señor Todas-Partes with an unlit cigarette in his mouth, laughing louder than anyone else after jokes, low-fiving friends and strangers, air-pistolling imaginary targets. All long strides and billowing shirts. Once or twice, while passing his group as they ate lunch and played poker, I thought I heard him call out my name, De! Vries!, as if he wanted me to join them, but I didn't think he was serious so I pretended I didn't hear him, until one day after school the hallway around our lockers emptied and it was just Dirk and me packing to go home. As I knelt to zip my knapsack, I looked over at him. Though most of his face was obscured I saw the corner of his mouth curling in a smile.

"She said you taught her everything she knows," he said.

"Who?" I said.

Dirk turned to me. "*Who*? Man, I should give you more credit."

He let out a loud laugh and I smiled, almost against my will.

"See ya, de Vries. I mean, Vries de." He banged on his locker door twice and walked away. Back hunched, feet splayed, snapping fingers like he was keeping beat with a drum solo.

I rode home feeling shaken and excited, my bicycle wheels barely touching the ground. In my head I was hearing the *Gnossiennes*, but at a slightly sped-up pace, and as I looked around I could almost see notes vibrating from tree branches and rippling across the surface of canals. A grace note broke like a twig under my tire. Triads radiated across the tall stalks in the fields and into the shadows in the forest. Every so often I'd get the sense Dirk was riding next to me, and I'd swing my head, right and left, to catch a glimpse. In my imagination he was watching the path of the music with me, already cracking jokes about it. Lovely *twigs*, de Vries. Clever run of *bark*.

Soon Dirk was shouting my name like a fanfare down the halls, giving me shots in the arm, cupping the back of my head as if I'd scored an important goal. He made space for me in his lunchtime circle and introduced me as "Ludwig von van der Vries" to Pym and Pirm and to girls, too, like Rika and Grietje, and others from his drama class and the years above. Like we had been friends for ages and I'd just reappeared.

At first I thought it might be a way for him to confound his friends, hanging out with the guy whose girlfriend he'd stolen. But then he started inviting me to his house after school. Initially with Beate and Pirm. Then with Pirm. Then just me, alone, almost every day. Hanging out together became our thing. Soon it was the only thing. I'd spend the day waiting for last bell, when Dirk and I'd meet at the bike racks and ride off together.

Dirk's mission during the rides home was to see if he could destroy his bicycle. Without warning he would fly ahead then jam the brakes, leaving long black streaks on the pavement. He called them "crapstains." The darker the better. When riding along a canal's edge, he swivelled his handlebars as if losing control. He was spectacularly bad at popping wheelies but that didn't stop him from trying. Each time he'd fall off the back of his saddle as the bike shot skywards.

"Piece of shit," he'd say, examining a snapped fender or derailed chain, "I can't help it's a piece of shit."

For Dirk, the more histrionic the wipeout the better. And because I tucked my hems into my socks and slowed down through puddles and tried not to ride off the side of dykes into canals, Dirk called me "Old Man," "Sobriety de Vries," and sometimes just "Arthritis."

"All right, de Vries," he said to me one day. "If you won't do any good tricks, you can at least ride eyes closed."

I thought to myself, I knew you were wild, but not crazy.

"No chance," I told him.

"Come on. I do it all the time."

"So I'll lay flowers at your grave."

He tsk-tsked. "You're soft, de Vries. First thing, you look ahead and calculate the distance to the next turn or bridge or whatever obstacle. Then you steady your speed, so you know how much time you have. Finally, you close your eyes and start to count. One, two, three. No rushing through the numbers! My record's twelve."

He squinted into the distance and moved his lips to show he was calculating. Then he said, "Okay," closed his eyes, and adjusted his grip on the handlebars. Not sure what to do, I biked next to him and kept count. One, two, three. He bobbed his head. He bit into his lower lip. Four, five, six. I held my breath.

I kept thinking he was going to ride into a fence or signpost or tree, but he had a knack for landing on grass, or at least the softer gravel, after which he'd get back on his bike and laugh.

"One day, de Vries, I'm going to break every single bone in my face, *and it's going to be great*. Now, your turn."

Somehow he persuaded me. The first few times, I kept my eyes closed for barely five seconds. I'd imagine my tires sliding along the gravel shoulder, or being caught short by a sewer grate. I'd start screaming and begging Dirk to warn me if I was heading towards a pole or off a bridge.

"No," he said, "but just to the right are shards of glass and barbed wire! And radioactive alligators! And a nuclear submarine!"

I'd snap my eyes open, convinced I would find myself face to face with the ground or hurtling over a dyke. Dirk would be miles ahead by then, looking back, his lower lip curled down. The look of pity.

"Your heart is too soft, de Vries!" he'd yell. "Yet we understand and are forgiving!"

When we got to Dirk's house, we'd lean the bikes against the magnolia in the centre of his garden. Then, as he opened the French doors that led to the kitchen, we'd begin to argue. Starting with our usual.

"You know I stole her from you," he'd say.

"Did not."

"So what are you saying, de Vries? That I *took out your trash?*"

Occasionally he would throw in a kind of twist. Frown. Turn his head to the side.

"She did say you were a primo kisser."

I'd narrow my eyes. "Well, I have had a bit of practise in my time," I'd say.

A poker face from Dirk. "I'm being serious."

For a moment it seemed possible.

"And also that you had *giant balls.* Like, elephantiasis of the testicles."

Dirk would laugh, duck out of the way, and throw things at me from cover. Fruit. A cookbook. A spatula.

"Come on, de Vries. Don't like what I said? Embarrassed by your boulder-like genitalia? Why is your eyelid twitching? Fancy having a go?"

He'd launch himself at me and get me in a headlock.

"I'm offering clemency under the Geneva Conventions, but you have to plead guilty to all charges."

Just as quickly as he'd pounce on me, he would let go, and begin to search for boxes of biscuits or mini waffles. Dirk's parents were almost always away, either on business in the city or on one of many trips out of town for his father's conferences. While Dirk slammed cupboard doors I'd collect my knapsack and remind him we needed to start on some homework.

"I know, I know," he said, shooting an imaginary gun at his temple.

"If you fail, they'll hold you back."

"Yes, I think I know how failing works."

"We'd be in separate grades."

"Well, then, you better get to work."

I'd transcribe answers into Dirk's workbooks while he, lounging on the bottom bunk stuffing biscuits down his throat, would start a new debate. Politics, usually. His parents called themselves left-wing, read *Het Parool* and got the *New Statesman* from England, and my father was always echoing the editorials in *NRC* and *De Telegraaf*. Getting into some kind of fight mostly meant parroting the opinions of our elders but with more gusto and insults, with Dirk threatening to put me in another headlock if he felt control slipping away. When the politics argument died without resolution, Dirk would choose one of the albums stacked above the stereo.

Dirk categorized his music by function. There was music for hanging out, music for going out, music for celebrating, usually funk, music for heartbreak, which was acoustic guitar with one singer. Most important was music for when you're with a girl. Percy Sledge, from America, was a leader in this category. "It Tears Me Up," "Warm and Tender Love." As the singer wailed, Dirk would sprawl across the bottom bunk and I'd sit next to him. He'd do the talking. I'd listen.

"Show me how you'd do it," he'd say.

I'd bunch three fingers together.

"No, no," he'd say. "You do it *this* way."

He'd take my ring finger away and flatten the index and middle fingers side by side. Next he'd put his palms together, thumbs in front, fingers facing down.

"Okay, now in."

I'd slide my two flat fingers between his palms, which gave slightly.

"See how much more comfortable that is?"

I'd nod, pretending to understand. Committing it to memory.

After a while he would get up from the bed and replace Sledge with another American, Aaron Neville, then lie back on the bottom bunk and put his hands behind his head. "Now *this* is music. *Soul* music. Not that Tchaikovsky ballet quartet shit you're always playing."

He'd puff his cheeks. Exhale. Stare at the mattress slats under the top bunk. Then he'd pick up an old thread. Beate, for example. He might be getting bored with her. He wasn't sure. What did I think? Oh, and did I see Horseface today? That was the name we gave to a girl two years older than us in the dance program, whose actual name we didn't know. She had short dirty blond hair and wild-looking eyes. The uniform shirt seemed tighter on her than on anyone else. Her nipples showed through.

"I saw her," Dirk said dreamily. "She was walking down the hall eating a *pickle*."

When the sky began to darken Dirk would see me off. Open the French doors to the garden, where I would lift my bike off his, and walk next to me to the top of the street.

Usually only in his socks or slippers, though the season was getting on.

"*A bientôt, mon petit!*"

He liked to swing around the stop sign post two or three times, a little *Dancing in the Rain*, then we'd embrace and I'd get on the saddle.

"Or maybe, de Vries, we shouldn't go to school tomorrow. Eh? Maybe fly away to Paris instead. Or Mombasa. Or Kinshasa. Or Lake Titicaca."

One time, or only one time that I can recall, I invited Dirk to my house. I did it under duress.

"My house is not fun," I said.

"Not fun *yet*," he answered. "But you have no idea what it *could* be. What I could make of it."

That was what I was worried about. It was one thing for Dirk to turn his house upside down, another thing for him to do the same to mine. What would my parents think of him? For one, he had no table manners. I loved this about him, of course. But on the occasions when our family ate together my parents were not shy about pointing out my infractions. And what about his foul mouth? I'd yet to even mutter the F-word in their company. What if Dirk sensed their dislike, and confused it for mine?

Then there was the other side. What if Dirk came to my house and saw I wasn't the person he imagined I was? What if he saw me for who I actually was, and decided I did not pass the test? He had cut off Lise overnight. What if he did the same to me?

He was persistent, though, so one day we met at the bike racks after school as usual, but instead of turning right at the end of the asphalt drive, we turned left. We followed the main road until we came to one of the rutty lanes that led past grazing fields.

The view opened. Rusty bathtubs that had been turned into troughs were set behind barbed-wire fences. Patches of grass sprouted irregularly from the chewed-up ground.

Dirk, who had been riding just behind me, stopped. He looked over the scene as though he hadn't been in the countryside for ages, even though he passed through it every day on his way to school. Milling in the distance was a flock of sheep, barely more than white fluff. Dirk stretched out his neck, fixed his lips like a trumpet's horn, and cut loose the most aggressive *Baa-aah* I'd ever heard.

We rode on. A few minutes down the road we approached a solitary goat, and Dirk's eyes widened. He straightened his arms, stood up on his pedals, and poured out a sound like a goat bleating into a megaphone.

"*Ghyuuuuuuuuuuuchhhh.*"

He turned to me. "Now try," he said.

"Try what?"

"Try *ghyuuuuuuchh.*"

I stood on my pedals and let out my best effort, which dissolved into a string of coughs. Dirk reached under his shirt, turned one of his nipples like a radio dial, and spoke into his chest. "We're going to need a better effort, roger, over."

We took turns riding with our eyes closed, counting out loud, pushing each other to make it to the next inter-section, bend in the road, bridge. When we got to edge of Vlijmen we instinctively knew it was time to race, and he and I fought for the lead through the roundabout, along the main road, right up to the driveway.

No one was at the house, and Dirk broke the stillness by emitting satyr sounds. We went upstairs to my room. Orderly, bright, spare—the opposite of Dirk's. When he saw my box of records at the foot of the bed he jumped towards it.

"Nice," he said, flipping through the albums, all classical. "I myself have great fondness for the Gherkin Polonaise." He stopped at the Enigma Variations by Edward Elgar, a version by the London Symphony Orchestra and André Previn, and examined the cover.

"Just *look* at the turtleneck on this fucker."

I snatched the album from his hands.

"Actually the B-side on this is amazing," I said. "Ralph Vaughan Williams' Fantasia on a Theme of Thomas Tallis."

Recently I'd been listening to it at very low volume every night before I went to bed. It was becoming a soundtrack.

"What's it like?" Dirk asked. "The so-called Fantasia?"

As usual, I couldn't tell if he was serious or kidding. I slipped the record from the cover.

"There's this mist of violas and cellos on one side, and a swarm of violins on the other. At first they're separate, off in their corners, but then they meet and become this big, shape-shifting, moving *thing*."

"Like a *rolling fog*?"

I ignored the comment, lay the record on the turntable, and switched on the stereo. The silence at the beginning of the recording dragged on. Then, finally, came the initial wave of strings. I felt a change in the atmospheric pressure. Dirk was with me at first, but he soon became restless.

"More like a pittering rain, Old Man."

I quickly lifted the needle and switched off the stereo, wary of more mockery.

"Or is it a *pattering* rain? A turgid wind? A disappointed riverbank? A nonplussed oxbow?"

Dirk stood up and began circling the room, revisiting certain pictures and objects as if he were looking for particular details.

"No, it's good, de Vries. I appreciate your geekiness. It's important. Valid. A *sclerotic bog* is what that piece is, actually." Then he looked directly at me. "I'm hungry. Is there anything to eat? Let's go check." He raced out of the room.

When I arrived in the kitchen I found him searching through cupboards, throwing doors open and clapping them shut two at a time.

"My stomach is crying, de Vries. Hunger in the midst of a first world nation."

When Dirk ran out of cupboards to open, his eyes went to the living room. I followed them as they fell on the piano. My piano.

"Dirk, no," I said, my voice rising.

He went over to it and ran his thumb under the Grotrian's rear lid, threatening to lift it.

"I wonder what's under here," he said. "I wonder if it's *cake*."

He rapped his knuckles against the frame, as if sounding the depths.

"Seriously, Dirk," I said. "This is not a good idea."

"Possibly, Old Man. But possibly it's a *great* idea."

He sat at the bench, quietly lifted the fallboard, and began to touch keys at random. *Tink . . . tink . . . tonk . . .* I froze, waiting for an explosion. But Dirk surprised me. Adjusting his posture, he hunched close to the keys and began to play softly, almost shyly. Single notes, intervals, repeated intervals, then again, with more confidence. A largo version of "Chopsticks." He shifted to the left side of the bench, making room for me.

"Don't be afraid, little one." I sat down and played the right hand, with improvisations, while he kept going with the elementary left.

After the piece petered out he stood up from the bench and requested a sad song. "Something morbid," he said, "or morbidly *obese*. A rolling, flatulent *dog*."

Against a soundtrack of "Morning Prayer," from Tchaikovsky's *Album for the Young*, Dirk performed a new, original work: "Soldiers Recently Returned from Front of Unspecified Twentieth-Century War, as Dramatized by the Documentary Division of Dutch National Television." He stooped from the edge of a kitchen stool as he spoke. His face barely registered emotion. Aside from musical direction, my job was to whisper the word "action."

"The Krauts are relentless . . . Their commander, Bratwurst von Mustardsauce, has ordered the entire battalion to burn every four-legged stool in a fifty-mile radius . . . We've held them off with nothing but toothpicks and dental floss, but I fear there may not be enough left over to get that bit of celery from the back . . ."

When my parents came home they insisted Dirk stay for dinner. We all ate together, which was unusual for weekdays, and my parents were in a good mood.

Dirk transformed himself into the perfect dinner guest. Napkin on lap, elbows down, holding fork by handle not tines, not interrupting my parents, never coming close to swearing. He took seconds. He accepted my father's offer of a sip of Scotch after dessert. He complimented my mother's cooking and, really winning her heart, cleared the dishes despite her protests.

When cleanup was over and Dirk had thanked my father and kissed my mother on the cheek, I walked him to the corner. As soon as we were out of sight of the house, Dirk's hunch returned. The loping strides. The fiddling with his ear. The sly smile.

"Thanks," I said.

"For what?" he said. "You were the one who graced me with the invitation."

"You know what I mean."

Dirk tilted his head, as if he heard a sound in the distance. Then he came back to the present.

"So," he said, "my place tomorrow?"

"Obviously."

"Goddamn right."

He got on his bike.

"*Mañana*, Old Man."

I 'd passed. Not that I stopped trying to prove myself, but, from then on, I felt he would give me the benefit of the doubt. After that one visit to my house we stuck to his. And as the term wore on I stayed in Den Bosch later and later.

I remember the first time I spent the night. It was a Friday and Dirk's parents were out of town for the weekend, which was common. Without his parents' arrival hovering over us, the house seemed larger and stranger. Dirk made use of the extra room by filling it with whoops and hollers. Instead of wrestling in the kitchen, we went to the living room, where Dirk slid the couch out of the way to make a mini arena.

"*Gladiatorum res gestae.* This time I'm putting one hand behind my back, but only because two would be an insult."

As I sat on the floor afterwards, rubbing my neck from the headlock, Dirk suggested I stay for dinner.

"We have an extensive menu. We'll eat on my parents' bed, watch television, then do something else. I don't know what. I haven't thought that far ahead."

I hesitated. I wanted to stay. I had heard Pirm talking about the legendary sleepovers. Cigars. Drugs. Pym, who had been standing by, nodded at everything Pirm said.

Still, I was supposed to be home for dinner. That was the deal I'd struck with my parents.

"Friday nights, you know."

"*Exactly*," Dirk said.

"I don't get it."

"Jesus of Nazareth, de Vries. Tomorrow's Saturday. No school."

I hesitated. Dirk whistled a long descending note. The sound of a plane in a tailspin. Then *krrrrrrr-schhhhhh*. The plane crashing nose first into the ground.

"Okay, okay," I said.

"Only *okay*, de Vries?"

"Yes, sir. Thank you, sir, Dirk, sir. Kindly pleased to stay for dinner."

I told him I just had to call my parents. He said I should explain that he was alone in the house, his parents were out of town, and that although it wouldn't technically be my fault if he was murdered in his sleep or had his *testonies* cut off by intruders or pirates, it would nonetheless haunt me for the rest of my life, and I should therefore stay overnight.

"Say that word for word, okay, Old Man? Do you need me to repeat it? Do you know what a *testony* is? Should I write this down for you?"

My father asked me what time I'd be home tomorrow, that was all. Dirk seemed to have anticipated the good news because he scooted out of the room as soon as I hung up and came back a second later clutching eight beer bottles against his chest.

"Time to start the party."

"Where'd you get those?"

"The Cask of Amontillado. Also known as my dad's liquor cabinet."

"And it's okay? To take this?"

"Okay? These are three-hundred-year-old beers brewed by three-hundred-year-old monks on top of some hill in France, or something. It's *definitely* okay."

"Dirk. Seriously."

"Seriously, de Vries. Se-ri-ous-ly. There's stuff in that cabinet from the twelfth century. Dust, actually, but still."

He winked, held a bottle to the corner of the little kitchen table in the bay window, and brought his fist down on it. The cap shot across the room. He opened another and handed it to me. Then he went to the sink and filled a cauldron-sized pot with water and set it on the stove.

Having downed his first beer, Dirk opened two more and giggled as he rapidly took sips. When the water reached boiling, he spilled in what looked like two kilograms of pasta and set a timer. We went back to the beers, Dirk making sure I was keeping up before sending another round of bottle caps flying. When the timer rang, Dirk drained the pasta into a colander and doused it in butter, salt, pepper, and cheese.

"*Primo, pasta con fasta. Secondo, rigatoni ecce romano!*"

I could barely break a quarter of the portion he served, and Dirk soon felt similarly sick, but proud of it. After a while we gave up on food altogether and Dirk knocked open the last of his father's beers.

"*Prost,* de Vries!"

That one went straight to my head. I felt like I was swimming, and Dirk must have been feeling it too, as wet gobs of rigatoni arced off the end of his fork into the general vicinity of the sink.

"Just trying to clean up, you know."

"What about the plan to watch TV in your parents' room?" I asked.

"I didn't forget," Dirk said, tapping his head with his finger. "But I have a better idea. Come."

He raced up the stairs and I stumbled after him, unbalanced by the drink. Next thing I knew he was racing back down, past me.

"Go ahead. I'm going to get a few more beers."

Dirk's room was in form. Homework from that day, the day before, and the year before was piled on the desk like garbage. Both cupboard doors were wedged open. Clothing overflowed from the shelves inside. Dirk appeared behind me, passed the beers, and held up his finger.

"Back in one second."

I heard him rummaging in his parents' room. I put the beers on the desk and went to the bookshelf. Maybe it was having climbed the stairs, but the sense that my brain was swimming in alcohol had softened. I could read the small-print titles of the records on Dirk's shelves. George Clinton. Parliament-Funkadelic, whatever that meant. The

O'Jays, which Dirk said was a present from his brother, who was in university in England. Archie Bell and the Drells, which Dirk had on regular rotation.

*Hi, everybody. I'm Archie Bell and the Drells, from Houston, Texas. We don't only sing but we dance just as good as we want.*

Next to the records were stacks of photographs. I picked one up and sifted through. Pictures of a younger Dirk. Paler. Shorter hair, though still unruly. The front tooth already chipped. On the shelf above the records and photos were books. Some were required reading from school, which Dirk took to mean voluntary. *War and Peace. Death in Venice*, which was probably where he kept a copy of Bushwoman. But most of them were the sci-fi paperbacks he collected. Almost all Frank Herbert. *Dune, Dune Messiah, Children of Dune, God Emperor of Dune, Heretics of Dune,* and *Chapterhouse: Dune*.

The sound of Dirk's lazy, dragging footsteps came down the hall, and I turned to see him standing in the doorway, holding his parents' TV set, which had a built-in video cassette player.

"Special delivery, de Vries. Please sign."

He used a foot to clear some space on the floor in front of the bottom bunk. He placed the television down carefully, at least for him, and ran the cord to the outlet under his desk. Next he went to his closet and, after rooting in the back, pulled out a grey gym bag, the kind everyone had in elementary school, knotted at the top.

He held it out to me. "All yours."

He watched as I undid the knot.

"I wonder what's inside, de Vries." His voice was taunting, but he was smiling.

I felt my heart start to beat. I *knew*, somehow, from something Pym had said, or the way Pirm looked, that Dirk was including me in some kind of special, Dirk-patented plan. When I pulled my hand out I saw I was holding a videocassette. The cover showed two women wearing bras, stockings, frilly panties, and fresh white caps with red crosses on them. One had a stethoscope hanging around her neck. The other was holding a needle and looking directly at me.

"De Vries? Hello? Don't tell me you've seen this one already."

I was silent. Dumb.

"Do you like the German ones?" he asked.

"Where did you get this, Dirk?"

"I have a subscription. Kidding. Sisi gave it to me. Actually Sisi bought it for me. And by me, I mean you. I told her it was your birthday and this is what you really, really wanted."

Sisi, with the enormous breasts. Two years older than us. Did she even know who I was?

Dirk took the case from my hands and pointed to the cupboard. "Somewhere in there are pyjama bottoms. Find two pairs. Can't be wearing school pants in bed!"

I changed in the corner with my back turned. Dirk knelt in front of the TV, pushing various buttons. He then propped two big pillows on the bottom bunk.

"Here you go," he said.

I pressed my back into one of the pillows and pulled the blanket up to my waist. Adjustments complete, Dirk sat back onto the pillow beside me and, under the covers, wriggled out of his underwear and into the pyjama bottoms.

"Ready?" he asked.

I nodded.

"Oh yeah," he said. "One last thing."

He got up, went to the door, and turned off the overhead lights. In the dark he shuffled to the corner, where I could hear him fiddling with a knob. Another click, and this time a thin beam shot up the blue-green wall, giving the room an underwater glow. "*Mood*," Dirk said.

He knelt by the side of the bed, pulled the cassette from the case, and slipped it into the video player. The screen went blue. We waited. An impatient Dirk leaned forward, smacked the side of the TV and stabbed the buttons. "Damn, fucking," he said, laughing. A nervous laughter. Unusual for Dirk.

Finally some combination of buttons worked, and the video began to play. After a moment of hesitation, Dirk lay back on the bunk. His heels bounced up and down on the carpet. His fingers drummed the blanket. A grin started to show on his face and he let out a small, beer-scented burp. The nurses appeared on screen. There were three, and except for their white gloves they were dressed as on the cover. A male patient entered the scene. One nurse looked at the other, then addressed the patient.

"Please remove your undergarments, sir," she said, in a dubbed voice.

I tried to focus on the scene but out of the corner of my eye I saw Dirk's hand under the duvet, shadows rippling across the surface.

After a second of hesitation, I slipped my hand under the covers and started to masturbate alongside Dirk.

"See the way he's doing it?" Dirk said, pointing with his free hand at the screen.

I looked briefly at the flickering picture but couldn't tell what he was pointing at. My attention was split. Part of me was watching Dirk, trying to see how fast he was going. How hard he was concentrating.

After a few more scenes he shuffled forward and pressed Pause, then sighed theatrically as he lay back into the pillows and stretched his arms to the side, as if he were swinging on a hammock. He flashed a smile.

"Perfect."

I looked at the clock on the stereo. It was midnight. Dirk got up from the bunk and went to his records.

"Did you finish?" he said, laughing. He didn't wait for an answer. "And now, for some music."

He had something new, he said, pulling out an album I didn't recognize. After slipping out the record, he handed me the cover. All it said was the name of the band, no album title. The Velvet Underground, which didn't make sense, if "velvet" and "underground" meant what I thought they did. On the back was a picture of a man smoking a cigarette. His collar was sticking out of his sweater. The new fashion.

Dirk set the needle on the record and slipped back into bed. I watched as the needle rolled slowly over the undulating vinyl, like a tiny boat riding long waves. At first there was nothing but the hum of the speakers. Then came a guitar, strumming out of time and out of tune. And a person singing, between whisper and falsetto.

Dirk lay back and cradled his head in his hands.

"Brilliant, eh?"

As I listened to the guitar, slowly falling into rhythm, my eyelids grew heavy. I drifted in and out of sleep, like the needle that rode the undulations of the record.


"De Vries . . . are you awake?"

I rubbed my eyes and face. The feeling of drunkenness was gone from my head. I could think clearly enough. The music had stopped but the hum of the speakers was still brushing my ears. I squinted at the green numbers on the stereo. One fifteen.

Next to me, Dirk propped himself up on an elbow and shifted onto his side. I did the same, facing him. Dirk moved closer to me, and after a second or two, I moved closer to him. I was so close I could feel the warmth rising from his chest. We didn't speak, and I don't think I even breathed. When I felt his hand on my back, I put my hand on his. Then he sank into the pillow and closed his eyes, and I sank down and closed mine.

After a while I realized I was breathing again, that we were breathing in the same rhythm. We stayed facing each other, eyes closed, chests rising and falling in unison, until we fell asleep.

D irk had taken it for granted that I'd be coming to his house for Christmas dinner, so he never bothered to actually invite me. When he finally got around to informing me of my expected time of arrival, I told him my parents probably expected me to go with them, to the neighbours'.

"So tell them you've got a better invitation," he said. "Who are your neighbours, anyway? I've never heard you mention them."

"The Zoetmulders."

"Oh, wait a second. The *Zoetmulders*?" he said, raising his arms in front of him, as though shielding himself from a radioactive blast. "My goodness, de Vries, why didn't you say right away it was the *Zoetmulders*? No right-thinking person would miss a chance to go to the *Zoetmulders*'."

I was about to launch a comeback when he cut me off.

"Too late for the Zoetmulders, Old Man. I've already told my parents you're coming, so you're coming. *Fait accompli*."

A week later, my mother was driving me to Dirk's. And though his house already felt like home to me, and I'd met his parents, this night was different. I was being inducted into the family. I had dressed in a crisp white shirt, navy sweater, wool pants, dress socks, and vigorously shined brogues. My most adult self.

When the car pulled up at the dead end in front of Dirk's I checked myself briefly in the reflection of the windshield. My mother handed me a wrapped a box of chocolates. "For Dirk's *parents*," she said, "not Dirk."

She probably added something else, but I wasn't paying attention. I'd caught sight of the kitchen, so brightly lit through the bay window, and was looking at the action inside. Though I hadn't met most of the people there, I felt I knew who they were from Dirk's descriptions. There was Dirk's parents, Wim and Cornelia, his older brother, his grandmother, who drank everyone's wine when they weren't looking. And another couple his parents' age, who must have been their regular Christmas guests, the Polhemuses. All crowded around the island, drinking, prepping food, talking, gesturing. Casual, belonging.

I kissed my mother goodbye, crossed the street, and skipped up the red brick steps to the glass vestibule in front of the house. The smell of sugar and brandy thickened the air. I rang the doorbell and listened. There was a pause in the noise from the kitchen, the shuffling of feet on tile, the scrape of the lock, and the turn of the brass doorknob. The door opened, letting out more brandy and sugar and the buttery smell of pie crust. I saw an oversized Christmas tree, which had taken over the living room. I heard jazz playing loudly. A voice like and unlike Dirk's, which must have been his brother's, was explaining something about

Athenian history. And before me, in the doorway, was Dirk's mother, Cornelia. "Master Jan has graced us with his presence," she said. "The little pianist has arrived!"

This was the cue for footsteps to come galloping down the stairs and socks to slide across the living room's waxed hardwood floor. Dirk, on the edge of control, came crashing into me, grabbing on to me not to fall. Then he stood up, put his arm around my shoulder, and without missing a beat said, "I believe you mean *Masturbator* Jan, the *little penis.*"

His mother threw her head back and laughed silently, a hand hanging in mid-air. Dirk imitated her, hanging his hand in mid-air.

After introductions and aperitifs, everyone moved to the dining room, where throughout dinner Dirk put on a bravura performance of Dirkness, and the entire family showed their unlimited adoration of everything he did. His father beamed. Granny stroked the back of his hand. The Polhemuses' niece, who arrived late and sat next to Dirk's brother, giggled at every one of Dirk's dirty punchlines. All of this was played around a table packed with food, so much, and so rich, and under a giant painting of a dog sleeping on a lush bed of purple grass—an "early Scholte," I had been told.

Time was only called when Wim, at the head of the table, unbuckled his belt, unbuttoned his fly, hung his head, and closed his eyes. By that point Granny had been led to a guest room at the back of the house, the Polhemuses had left, and Dirk's brother and the Polhemuses' niece had gone off somewhere.

"You two boys go to the tree," Cornelia said in a wobbly voice. "I'll manage the plates."

I stumbled to the living room couch. Dirk, riding another of his second winds, threw his father's old newspapers into the low-burning fire and grabbed hold of the poker. I rested my eyes for a moment only to be hit in the head by a flying object.

"*Vorsicht*, de Vries," Dirk said, unwrapping the gift that landed next to me on the couch—the gift I'd brought. "And what could this be?"

"It's for your parents," I said.

"That's just going to make them taste better, Old Man."

Dirk rubbed his hands and opened the box, which contained dozens of individually wrapped chocolates set in a grid. He pulled out chocolates at random, unwrapped them, took small bites from each, then rewrapped the uneaten portions and placed them back in the box. "Funny," he said. "They all taste the same."

He snapped the box shut and threw it aside, knocking other presents and tinsel dangerously close to the fire. "Feel like ducking upstairs," he said, "and watching an interesting mature video?"

I looked into the kitchen. "Your mother's right there," I hissed. "She can probably hear us!"

"Good point, de Vries. It'd be rude not to extend the invitation."

Dirk cackled at his joke, drew a breath, and bolted up the stairs two at a time. I sprang to my feet and raced after him.

"I'm going to beat you up, de Vries," Dirk called back at me, not caring who heard.

If Dirk and I were inseparable before, then that first Christmas, the first of four I spent at his house, showed we were bonded in a new way. We had become best friends. A circle of two, into which no one else was admitted.

During the years at Sint Ansfried, I must have had my own classes, spent time alone practising, spent lunches by myself, and I remember leaving Dirk's house on Saturday afternoons, which means I must have spent the rest of the weekends away from him. But I cannot pick out a memory from those years that does not find Dirk by my side. We spent what felt like years at the movie theatre, sitting through many bad and terrible movies. We listened to experimental music in record shops and in his room and went to watch bands play in bars and small clubs. We walked every street in Den Bosch, where he lived, and Vught, where we cut classes, something we did with increasing frequency, ducking out of math and languages and going to sit in a café to talk, argue, laugh.

There's a stack of photographs, letters, and postcards I collected from those years that I've crammed into a shoebox, and I can call up almost all of them by heart.

There is the picture I took of Dirk in art class, wearing a paint-smeared smock and wielding a paintbrush like a fencing foil. Another that Dirk took of me after six months of growing out my hair in grade eleven, transforming myself into a kind of Shirley Temple with a dirty upper lip.

There's a picture of Dirk and me standing at the edge of the sea on a class trip to Zeeland. Both of us with pants rolled above the knee, wading into the water. Dirk is wearing a tricorne hat bought at a thrift shop in Middelburg, windblown wavy hair sticking out the back. He bought me a hat too, a type of a beanie, and made me wear it. The entire trip, even on the train ride back, he insisted on being called Louis Napoleon Matador.

"Louis Napoleon the *Third*, mind."

There's a picture taken from the bay window of Dirk and me playing soccer in the park. Dirk's hair corralled by a terrycloth headband, a plastic ball at his feet, a look of intensity on his face as he is about to dribble past me. There is a particularly memorable photo of Dirk and me dressed up for the Graduation Ball, all pomp and pomposity. I'm in a rented tuxedo and Dirk's in a velour smoking jacket bought from the charity shop in downtown Den Bosch. My hair is combed forward to hide a nasty job I'd made of trying to get rid of a pimple, and Dirk's square-framed sunglasses are hanging off the tip of his nose. I'm smiling with closed lips; Dirk's leering at the camera and, on close inspection, showing a hint of the chipped tooth.

As for the letters and postcards, I know these by heart too.

The note Dirk mailed from Den Bosch on a Tuesday afternoon that got to me in Vlijmen on Wednesday morning. "I am bored. What are you up to tonight?" The letter from France, where he spent part of a summer. "Dear Mister de Vries, We, at the ministry of completely irrelevant things, would like to remind you that the Bengal Tiger is not native to Paris. Furthermore the Bengal Tiger will not be found in the middle of the Pacific Ocean." There is a crumpled bill taped to the bottom left-hand corner of the postcard. An arrow leads to a tightly scrawled explanation. "Ten francs folded five times equals two francs, it seems."

There is a scribbled message from the other side of a class. "Hello young sir, Hello and welcome to this letter. I am theoretically in class right now, though if I were to be strictly accurate, I would say that is a vast overstatement." That one is signed, "I hate you, I love you," each struck through, followed by "You are okay."

There is the drawing he made for Sint Ansfried's improvisational theatre show, *Thespus*. Dirk drew brilliantly, often making sketches of imaginary and imaginatively hairy animals with surplus legs, clublike tails, and claws that gripped smaller, flailing versions of themselves. He could turn out masses of those animals, great populations of them. For the show's poster, he drew two shaggy-haired creatures interlocked in mortal embrace, with one of the animals calling to the other, "Cry mercy!" Which was what Dirk always said when he had me in a headlock or was twisting an arm behind my back.

"Cry mercy, de Vries! Cry mercy, Old Man!" His forearm cutting farther into the neck. My shoulder being pulled nearly out of its socket. "Say it, Jan! *Mer-cy!*"

People at school treated those posters like collector's items, tearing them from the walls as soon as they appeared. When the show was over, Dirk gave me the original, in blue ink. "I made it for us," he said.

That was Dirk and me in public: what others knew, and could see. But there were also things we didn't talk about, not even to each other. The things we couldn't explain, but just did.

Like the times we argued or joked or horsed around, this also followed a routine. It started Friday afternoons, when Dirk and I would cut the last class, ride to central Den Bosch, hang out in record stores and go to the movies. The first couple of years we'd cap the outing with a slice of pizza or hot dogs and fries, complemented with beers from his father's cellar at home, but as we got older we'd stop for a drink in a pub or head out to a house party when someone's parents were out of town. If it was a big night, Dirk and I'd get drunk and smoke a joint that Dirk would buy, usually off Pirm. If our adventure took us far, we'd leave our bikes behind, locked to a fence, and Dirk would call a cab to take us back, happy to pay, because while I had a two-guilder-a-week allowance, Dirk got thirty and didn't care about money. He loved letting coins spill out of his pockets, leaving them where they fell on the pavement.

When we got home at two or three, we'd stumble into the kitchen. The sink would sometimes be full of dishes, but the little table in the bay window was always clear enough that I could rest my head on it as I slumped into a chair. Even though Dirk had likely drunk twice as much as I had, he'd shuffle to the shelves near the sink, find two glasses, and run the tap till the water was cold.

"It'll take the edge off, Old Man."

We'd drink glasses and glasses of water, till I'd start feeling my stomach pressing against my belt. Then we'd make our way to the stairs where, ever since I had taken a fall on one of our first nights together, Dirk would dutifully follow me up, ready to catch me in case I did an encore.

The lights in his room would already be dimmed, and I'd amble between piles of clothes and books to the mattress, focusing most of my thoughts on not hitting my head against the top bunk. As I lay sideways among the scattered pillows, the world would spin anew, but as soon as Dirk joined me, it slowed, then grew still.

As we lay side by side, Dirk would say something about a girl at a party or the girl he was going out with at the time, about how he had gone down on her. He would add advice. Pay attention to her breathing to know if she's liking it. Keep the same rhythm once you've found the sweet spot. Do not change technique if you think you're getting close.

At some point, I would notice music playing in the background. Dirk always had something set up on his turntable, but I only noticed the sounds when he and I stopped talking. It was the old songs we used to listen to, only quieter. A slow bass. A lonely voice singing about love. A guitar edging in and floating out.

As I tried to pick the strands apart, Dirk would begin unbuttoning his shirt, but more often than not he'd grow impatient and lift it, half-unbuttoned, over his head. I'd get under the covers and wiggle out of my underwear. A shirtless Dirk would stand up, walk to the door, and turn off the lights. In the darkness I would hear him come back to the bed and feel him pull at the covers. As my eyes adjusted to the street light that seeped under the drawn curtains I could make out the shape of his head, neck, and shoulders, and see that he was facing me. Listening to the shallow sounds that emanated from the speakers, moving in and out of earshot, I tensed for the moment when he would shift in the bed. That would be the signal. He'd prop himself up, inch closer, and I'd do the same. I'd feel a hand on my side, above the hips. I'd put my hand in the same place above Dirk's hips. He'd move his hand down, between my legs. I'd do the same.

Dirk would always finish first and when he did, he'd shiver slightly. Then he'd push me onto my back to finish me. I'd close my eyes and concentrate. The music would mix with the sound of his breathing. One of his hands would sometimes press on my chest, his knee might brush the inside of my leg. When I was done, Dirk would let out a short laugh, wipe his hand on the sheets, and pull the covers over himself. We'd lie like that, side by side, just the sounds of the wind outside and whatever music was still murmuring from the speakers. Somewhere between five and ten minutes, always side by side. Until our breathing went back to normal.

When Dirk moved, raising his head or shifting onto his side, that would mean it was time to wash up. We'd slip out of bed, sneak down the hall to the bathroom, and huddle at the sink to share the running water. I'd tilt to one side, Dirk to the other. We'd use hand towels to dry off. I'd fold mine and hang it off the rack when I was done. Dirk would usually drop his on the floor.

In the dark we'd find our way back to bed and under the duvet. Sometimes we'd sleep facing each other, like on that first night. Other times he'd hold me from behind. It always took a few minutes to get comfortable. To adjust the pillow, stretch a leg out for a cool patch of mattress, use a free hand to pull at the covers, and to let the other know he was still awake. Then we were quiet. The last track on the record would play out, in reality or imagination. The eyelids would droop, and the body drowse.

In the morning we'd wake up across the mattress from each other and it was as though the previous night hadn't happened. We'd get out of bed, throw on pyjamas and housecoats, head down to the kitchen, and talk about girls, parties, music, movies, and the future, especially as we approached graduation, escape from Sint Ansfried, and entrance to the wide world.

"We're going to be *fat*," Dirk would say.

"Fat," I repeated.

"I'll be fat from always being on the move, bouncing from place to place, putting on productions wherever I can scrounge out a stage. One day I'll have my name in lights, an Oscar in my hand. The next I'll be in obscurity, in a clearing in a forest, in front of people who speak strange languages. I'll go from riding first class to hanging off the back of a bus. From suites at the George Cinq to a dirt floor under a leaking tarp. I will suffer from tapeworm and have to drink a poisonous juice made from local berries."

I'd smile. "And me?"

Dirk would press a finger to his lips and give me a serious look. "I've thought about this, de Vries." He'd frown, wrinkle his forehead. "You'll be chubby, Old Man."

"Only chubby?"

"Okay, you're right. You'll be *lardaceous*."

Dirk would grab my hand and look at the lines of my palm, or slurp the last of his coffee and stare at the grounds.

"You and I, de Vries, will be like two cans of lard sitting on the same shelf. One shopper will throw me into her cart, another will throw you into hers. I'll be donated to a local food drive, the world never knowing my true identity, and you'll be whisked to the pantry of an English manor and baked into the crust of a love-and-marriage quiche, filled with the cream of haut bourgeois existence. You'll give concerts in the finest salons, playing Tchaikovsky ballet string quartets on the piano, and have your face on the cover of a Deutsche Grammophon record. I'll be fat from eating fast food and the piles of trash that gather at the crossing of two highways. You'll be fat from a steady diet of venison and cognac."

"Fat people die young," I'd say.

"*We* will live till the age of wisdom," Dirk would answer. "One hundred years old. Each."

"So we'll have a weigh-in at fifty?" I'd ask.

"Yes," Dirk would nod. "And all this terrificness will start for you, Old Man, in Maastricht. I can already see you under stage lights. New York City, Los Angeles, Paris. Flying first class where they have wider seats, because you'll be *fat*."

In December of my last year at Sint Ansfried, I applied to the de Groot Conservatory in Maastricht, the finest music academy in the Netherlands. Dirk had been the technician for my audition tape and even proofread, without too much mocking, my application essay on the influence of Eastern instruments on Debussy's sonatas.

Dirk's applications, which were all to schools in America, involved a live audition in Amsterdam in February. In the lead-up to the date, he rehearsed maniacally, subjecting me to multiple variations on a series of monologues, but when the day came he took the train up north like it was no big deal and returned the next day with a bunch of typically Dirk stories. How his leg fell asleep during the Pinter and he had to Igor his way around the room. How he was helplessly attracted to the angora-sweatered breasts of one of the examiners, even if she was ninety-four years old.

I was accepted by Maastricht in mid-March. Dirk had to wait. But when he got the big envelope, during the last week of April, he brought it to school and opened it with me, at our lockers, at the end of the school day. There was a calendar with pictures of campus. A several-hundred-page course catalogue. Dormitory forms. Student visa forms. A bumper sticker for his parents' car. Dirk tried to act nonchalant, but I could see his excitement, his pride.

"This is only step one, a *minor corpulence*," he said. "All part of the larger plan to tear right through the asses of the pants we're currently wearing."

With our courses charted, school stopped mattering, and Dirk turned his attention to making one last splash. In grade nine he'd assistant-produced *Thespus*. In grade ten he was Hamlet, in *Dogg's Hamlet*. In eleven he was Gilgagorm in a one-act play he wrote called *Beowulf for Breakfast*. But for his send-off he wanted to do everything *at once*.

"I know what it is," he said. "*Gargantua Redux*."

Dirk had long talked about turning *Gargantua and Pantagruel*, required reading in grade ten, into a play. I'm not sure he'd actually read the novel, or even half of it, but he often recalled the bits he'd picked up about dirty monks, corrupt bishops, cloisters, drinking, war, rogering, swearing, codpieces, exotic animals, decapitation, floods of urine, and grand speeches to "the people," and was determined to transform it into a show.

"It'll be a demonstration of pure Dirkian nonsense," he said.

Somehow he persuaded the head of the drama department to give him the run of the studio. He wrote up a script and cast everyone from his class, Pym, Pirm, Beate, even Lise, putting himself in the lead, as Gargantua. He moved the story to a Japanese setting, included a silent chorus, and left stretches of dialogue in the original French. And in a grand gesture, he had an upright hauled onto the stage so I could play in the background through most of the action. "An original sequence," he promised. "It will be *Sprachgenie!*"

After some experimentation, Dirk and I settled on a Chopin mazurka, opus 7, no. 1. It would be introduced in the opening scene, with improvised variations during the rest of the play. At certain points, Dirk had the cast hum to the melody. He also decided I'd be in costume with everyone else, turning out the sunny mazurka while knives and threats and stuffed animals flew. We rehearsed for a week, Dirk frequently sitting on the risers, taking notes and offering encouragement.

"Oh . . . this is totally . . . fuck me . . . *yes.*"

After the final run-through on the day before opening night, the cast and crew assembled and Dirk made his prediction.

"People will hate it," he said. "They will get up from their chairs and leave. And I will be so proud of you."

The opposite happened. Sellouts extended the initial run of three days to a week. It was standing room only, and on the final night we were well over legal capacity. Dirk took his bows before an ovation given by students, parents, teachers, and people from Vught and Den Bosch.

The morning after the last show, Dirk and I went back to an empty Sint Ansfried to clear out our lockers, throwing away things we had kept for years. Unreturned textbooks and library books. Pieces of clothing, either moth-eaten or too filthy to bother cleaning. Cutlery once considered lost. A detailed sketch of testicles, which Dirk had drawn years before. He held the sketch to the light. "God, I'm good," he said, scratching the stubble on his chin before he crumpled the piece of paper.

We stumbled across a pornographic magazine that Dirk and I once thought we'd misplaced somewhere in his house. We'd spent a weekend tearing through every room, then decided to appease the gods by dumping the grey gym bag that carried our entire porn collection into a postbox on the corner.

Dirk flipped through the magazine, then tossed it over his shoulder, into the growing pile of garbage. "I wanted to say something to you, de Vries," he said, "and not about that magazine, which I do remember and which almost gave me a fucking heart attack."

He put his hand out, and we shook. I tried to look solemn but was unable. For the moment, though, Dirk seemed serious.

"I wanted to thank you," Dirk said, still holding my hand. "I don't know where I would've ended up if it weren't for you. I mean, I could have gone on the wrong path. Ended up like Pym, Pirm, all those guys. Nice people, but, you know. You kept me on track, de Vries."

I didn't know how to take his words, or answer them, so I stayed quiet. Eventually, Dirk let go of my hand.

"Now let's get the fuck out of here," he said.

We collected all our junk in a black garbage bag, which Dirk slung over his shoulder. On the way out, he kicked every door's push-bar, and I did the same.

That summer passed at presto tempo as Dirk and I compressed as many experiences as possible into four months. I must have spent every day at Dirk's and stayed over most weekends. Fridays we had our routine, and Saturdays we went to the park or bars downtown to meet friends or pick up girls. In mid-July a group of us drove to a fair in the countryside where they had set up a roller coaster that Dirk made me ride seven times in a row. "Until you puke," he said. "Until I can see your fucking lungs." In early August he had a fling with a girl who went to another school and I spent a weekend at home while the girl stayed at his house, but the next weekend we were back to normal.

Then came the end of the August, and Dirk's last party. We were supposed to set up together but I had a bad cold, which threw off the plans. On the way to Den Bosch I stopped at a pharmacy to fill a prescription and when I

showed up at Dirk's door my eyes were streaming and my
nose was stuffed.

"Oh, what are we going to do?" he said, half mockingly.
"Party through the pain, I guess."

I walked into the kitchen and put my overnight bag
on the floor. Every inch of the counter was covered with
bowls and bottles and pitchers and serving plates, each
filled or covered with food and drink. Cheesy Goldfish,
Ritz, Baken Snaps, Grasshoppers, and Pop Rocks. Wimp
and lemon-lime Fresca. Pigs in blankets, soft cheeses, two
dozen oysters, and ten bottles of cava, which Dirk called
"aspirational champagne." Dirk looked at the assembled
display as though he were seeing it for the first time himself,
and seemed impressed. "New Dirk, mature Dirk," he muttered to himself. He rolled his head back, then side to side,
and bounced on his feet, like a boxer preparing for a fight.

Dirk had had get-togethers, smaller parties, and even
dinner parties, but never an all-out bash, and he had great
ambitions. He started by drawing up a guest list, which
was actually a guest list of girls, specifically those he had
yet to score. First was Anna, from the year above us, who
had promised Dirk a "dry run" on his birthday. "That's
when the girl takes off all her clothes," Dirk had explained,
"and the guy takes off everything except his underwear.
The whole thing is she can touch you but you can't touch
her." Anna had made the promise at a cast party the year
before, but then she graduated. "Does graduation annul
such promises?" Dirk asked. "Difficult to surmise." But

she was still in town and friends with girls in his class, so she was invited. Same with Rika, an off-and-on standby for Dirk. He had never gotten that far with her, so she was the backup in case Anna went sideways. Then there was Pym, Pirm, and Beate, of course. We struggled with Lise. Dirk pointed out that she had gotten better looking since we dated her. She was now better looking than Stefa. She made the list.

By eight o'clock my medication was kicking in. Dirk and I went to his room where he had me try on clothes from his closet. We went through suit vests, open-collar shirts, striped pants, and brogues, and settled on flared jeans and an untucked, mustard-coloured dress shirt, sleeves rolled up. Vest on top of that? Sure. Bandana? We decided against. In the bathroom Dirk and I shaved in front of the mirror, then he fixed my hair with gel and doused us both with 4711 cologne. Before switching off the bathroom light, Dirk stared intently at his reflection, slapped his face twice, hard, and declared himself ready.

At around nine people started showing up, and by ten the volume on the downstairs stereo was at full blast. Despite the curated guest list, the party quickly became a free-for-all. People brought their own drinks and cigarettes and joints, which they ashed everywhere. The couch migrated. The carpet was flipped over. The oysters and strange cheeses were the only things that stayed intact.

Dirk, meanwhile, was in his element, revelling in how his party was getting out of hand, glad-handing people he'd never met before, letting out screams for no reason and at no one in particular. At a certain point he'd begun hugging old friends while mock crying, then stepping back and looking at them as though they were strangers. It was like a curtain call on the Sint Ansfried years.

At half past two I lost stamina. My ears were plugged and my head was foggy. More people had arrived after midnight, maybe coming from another party, and I lost track of Dirk in the crowd. I climbed halfway up the stairs, to survey the living room, and saw him sliding between groups of girls.

"Dirk!" I called. "*Dirrrrrrk!*" He didn't hear, but when I waved my arms, I caught his eye. I motioned that I was quitting for the night. He looked at me as if I couldn't be serious.

"But this is the last party, de Vries!"

I mimed that I was dying on my feet.

"I wouldn't be graduating if it weren't for you!" he yelled.

I shook my head and smiled.

"You're right! It's not true, de Vries! But I wouldn't be graduating *this year*! Stay up a little longer. It's your party, too."

I shot an imaginary pistol at my forehead. Who knew mixing cold medication with booze would be such a downer?

Dirk waved with two hands. "I'll be up . . . soon!"

I trudged the rest of the way up the stairs and undressed as soon as I got into Dirk's bedroom. Closing the door muffled some of the noise from downstairs, but not all of it. I felt restless, dizzy, and overheated as I collapsed onto the bottom bunk. The covers twisted themselves around my body. I closed my eyes and tried to keep them shut, but every so often, when I forgot I was trying to sleep, I opened them again and looked at the green numbers on Dirk's stereo. 2:52 . . . 3:12 . . . 3:28. Downstairs the music was still playing, and in the pauses between tracks, I heard glasses clinking, cupboards shutting, the front door slamming. At 3:47 I heard a large group leave. "Goodnight! Ta!" A brief silence followed, but then came another series of whoops and something or someone crashing to the ground. More laughing, more music, and Dirk's voice rising above the din.

It was well after four o'clock that the house fell quiet and the music stopped. I strained for the sound of footsteps padding up the stairs. I held my breath and listened closely. At first nothing. Then came something from downstairs. Dirk and Anna? The dry run?

The clock numbers blurred. My eyelids felt heavy. I shifted in bed trying to find a comfortable position to fall asleep. Not long after, I heard the door to the bedroom creak open. An outline of Dirk. Then the door closed.

He crawled onto the bottom bunk, beside me. Sitting on top of the duvet, facing me, he stripped off his pants and underwear. Even in the dark, and bleary-eyed as I was, I could make out his penis lying against one of his thighs. I propped myself against a pillow. Dirk got under the covers and put his hand flat on my chest. I lay back, closed my eyes. The world started to spin. I heard him

mumble something and felt him change position so that
he was leaning over me. I opened my eyes slightly, looked
down, and saw his head at my waist. I felt his breath on
my stomach. He eased the hand on my chest, telling me
to relax. Then he turned around to face the wall. *Do it, de
Vries.* I got on my knees and leaned over him. I felt his hand
take me inside. He grunted at first, then held his breath.
I held mine and pushed. I heard him exhale, letting me
know to keep going.

Dirk left for America. I left for Maastricht. All of a sudden I was faced with new surroundings, new classmates, new tutors, and practice routines. I was excited, and nervous. In the early days I'd get the sensation that Dirk was sitting in class with me, and if I'd glance over my shoulder, I'd see him. Sometimes, at the end of the day, I'd imagine telling him what I'd seen and learned and done, as if we were sitting on his bottom bunk, listening to music. Ray Charles, Booker T and the MGs. I thought of calling or writing, but somehow never got around to it. At the same time, neither did he, so I didn't feel like I was letting down the side. I figured we were both sorting through new surroundings and would save up our stories for Christmas.

There was plenty to tell. I had applied to the conservatory with full confidence, but when I got there I quickly saw myself as a dilettante surrounded by proper musicians. When I heard others play I realized I was not the standout I had been at Sint Ansfried. For many of the other students, performing was effortlessness, mastery a given. I was in a dinghy, rowing against the waves; they were on a motorboat, gliding over glassy waters. The laws of friction and inertia did not apply. Did they even need to practise?

But the thought of Dirk on the other side of the ocean, thriving in a more alien culture and different language, made quitting impossible. If he could do it, I could do it. And better.

So I made a decision: treat Maastricht like my new home. This would be my base, my foundation. The launching pad, as Dirk had described it. And yet I couldn't shake the habit of comparing the new to the old. Some laneway in Maastricht would remind me of one in Den Bosch. A new bar I'd visit was compared to an old one around the corner. The Maas river to the Den Bosch canals. New squares to old squares. Markets to markets, buildings to buildings, classrooms to classrooms. Same with the friends I was making. I opened myself up, but kept measuring new personalities against what I'd known, the regular crowd at Sint Ansfried. For the first time I had my days and nights to myself; no meals waiting for me at set places, no obligation to answer or need to explain myself to anyone. An open road ahead. Undefined and limitless. But any time I started to follow it, while taking a break from the keyboard or assigned reading, or lying in bed trying to fall asleep, it led me to a familiar place, as if on its own. Den Bosch. The end of the Grafstraat. Dirk's house. The morning after the big party.

It had started with Dirk shouting from downstairs. "Get up get up getup getup *get on up!*"

I sat up, my entire head feeling like a giant bruise. I remembered the previous night's drinking, the medication.

"It's a fucking dump site down here," Dirk went on, "and I didn't tell my parents I was having a party!"

Eventually I got up, and Dirk and I spent that morning cleaning, but not very quickly and probably not very well. Every time we stopped to survey the scene it was demoralizing. Clothes snagged on lights, glass shards caught in the carpet, wine-stained napkins and tablecloths spread around the kitchen, bits of food smeared across walls and on light switches. Dirk played *The Beatnik Years* quietly on the stereo while we did the scrubbing and wiping. We took turns using the vacuum, shutting it off every few minutes because it was loud. When we figured the main floor was clean enough we went upstairs to shave and shower. I spent more time brushing my teeth that day than I have any day since.

Dirk's parents came home in the middle of the afternoon with presents for him. Flannel and worsted pants, a blue blazer and sweaters for the "East Coast winter." Food for the flight over that included a box of chocolate-covered stroopwafeln. If they noticed lingering smells or the disinterested job we had done of tidying the house, they held their tongues. Dirk brought the goods upstairs and cracked open the box of stroopwafeln. As we ate them I asked him what the score was, after last night.

"Ahh, Anna," he said. "I remember two beautiful nipples and . . . it goes black." He pulled at his earlobe. "I know she wasn't wearing any panties. My head hurts."

The whole family had an early dinner in the dining room like old times, under the Scholte dog, and as Cornelia cleaned up I brought my overnight bag down, and shortly after we packed into the Noosens' car for the drive to Vlijmen, Dirk and I in the back. As the car left Den Bosch for the countryside Dirk began singing, "Arrrgh, me shanty," and belching. Wim, smirking in the rear-view mirror, lowered the windows a crack to clear the smell. Fresh air whistled in. Dirk tilted his head in thanks, "Arigato, Father-san, air and wind, Father."

I looked through the windshield to the road ahead. Arrow straight and perfectly flat. An ideal stretch of asphalt. I thought of all the days I'd biked along this stretch of road with my eyes closed. I had been back and forth to Dirk's so often, I'd memorized every dip and rise of the A2, every bridge and cross street. I had gotten so good I could *sense* my proximity to the shoulder. When I started on an especially straight stretch, like the one we were on now, I would shut my eyes and play a tune in my head, something I was working on at the time. A climb of octaves in a steady rhythm, the bottom note just touching the ground, music to distract myself from the fact I was riding blind. I'd start the count. Two, three, four. Seven, eight, nine. And just as I could see thirteen around the bend, the inside of my eyelids would glow from the headlights of an approaching car, real or imagined, and I'd snap my eyes wide open. I had been *so close*. And now I was leaving. When would I get another chance to top the record? I remembered telling Dirk I was getting close. Ten. Eleven. Twelve. He answered by mocking me. "You still play that silly game, Old Man?" But I could see he was impressed, maybe even jealous. "You'll never make it to thirteen, though. It's impossible."

"Wake up, Old Man!" Dirk snapped his fingers next to my ear. "We're nearly there."

The car passed the Vlijmen roundabout and was cruising down the main road. Dirk started shantying again, swinging his body left and right, his arm resting on my shoulder. At the playground the car made a left, then slowed as it snaked to the house. When it pulled up at the drive, Dirk jumped out and he and I walked to the front door.

"Fatness," Dirk said. "Corpulence. Total, all-consuming, diabetes-guaranteeing *obesity*." He gave me his chip-toothed grin. We hugged for a long time. "Onwards and upwards," he said into my ear. "And outwards. All at the same time."

I played that day back to myself dozens of times during my first term in Maastricht, a piece of music next to the ones I was meant to be practising. Then I'd snap back to the present. An uneven cobblestone street, the chatter of students picking up mail at the porter's desk, someone's door being closed across the dormitory hallway. Things that were gradually, despite some resistance, becoming familiar. But this still wasn't my real home. And while I stopped expecting Dirk to pop up at the desk beside me, or be at the bottom of the stairs in my dorm, he was still the best friend I had in Maastricht. I was anxious to go back and see him.

❖

Like everyone else on campus I left Maastricht on December twenty-third. I took the late-afternoon Intercity train, direction Amsterdam Centraal. It was the local, and more people were getting out than coming in. Soon I was the last person in my car. I moved next to the window and started searching the night sky for the vapour trails left by passing airplanes. As the train made its way into the familiar flat countryside, I followed the double lines as they lit up and faded in the large black bowl above. It was possible Dirk was on one of those planes. Gliding over the fingers of land that stretched into the sea, heading towards the banks of cloud that hover permanently above Amsterdam.

As soon as I could see Den Bosch, the nearest station to Vlijmen, my head began cycling through two pieces. Schubert's Sonata no. 21 in B-flat and Rachmaninoff's prelude in C-sharp Minor. I had started practising them at the beginning of the month and had played them so often they were lodged in my brain, playing themselves regardless of whether or not I was in front of a keyboard. The two pieces were natural opposites. The Schubert had the most beautiful opening of any piece I had played. As if the notes were balanced on the thinnest, most fragile wire. They ascend and descend, but every time you think the melody will break away, it returns to level. A buildup to forte, a return to mezzo. The introspective passages of pianissimo never dwelling long enough to grow melancholy. Underneath all that, a regular pulse of octaves in the bass clef gives the piece a steady and abiding feeling of hope.

The Rachmaninoff C-sharp, on the other hand, is a pack of limbs falling spectacularly down a flight of stairs. A tumbling that builds up to an explosion of chords, broken and solid, shooting up and sliding down octaves. The final section repeats the opening by doubling up the chords. Left and right hand cross over each other, the tempo increases until runs of notes crash in waves running crosswise. Dirk would like the Rachmaninoff. If he came to the house, to pick me up or drop me off, I would definitely play it for him.

The train got in around eight. The taxi quickly slipped out of Den Bosch and onto the quiet A2. A lining of hoar-frost covered the land, starting from the tall plants and reeds on the banks of the canal and spreading past the fields into the forests. Root, trunk, branch, needle. Soil, furrow, blade. All of it, from Den Bosch to Vlijmen, skinned in ice. One push, I imagined, and I could skate from one to the other.

In the morning I practised on the old Grotrian upright, mostly to impress my parents. My father sat on the couch next to the piano and, for old time's sake, brought his work with him and made passing comments on my playing.

When I took a break from my pieces, I stretched my fingers with technical exercises. Scales and formulas. Chords, broken and solid. Arpeggios, major, minor, harmonic, melodic. When I ran out of permutations I took out Czerny's School of Velocity and opened to a random page. I used the metronome to work my way through the tempi. Andante, moderato, allegro, presto, prestissimo. Faster and faster,

turning the drizzle of notes into thunderstorms. A spasti-
cally bravura performance. With nothing more to show,
and believing the Czerny might be irritating my father, I
spent the afternoon fitting puzzle pieces with my mother
and cracking the spine of the Glenn Gould biography that
had been assigned reading. After that I looked through the
syllabus for the upcoming term. Ives' tone pieces, Galina
Ustvolskaya's forceful, blocky preludes.

Towards evening I allowed myself to look at my watch.
Christmas dinner was twenty-four hours away. Less, if you
counted aperitifs and truffle rolling. The obvious course of
action would have been to pick up the phone and dial Dirk's
number, but I couldn't bring myself to do that. Between
the two of us, Dirk had always been the one to pick up the
phone, initiate the plan. I thought that maybe this was a
kind of test. Who could hold out longer. If so, I'd spent a
term waiting. I could last another day.

To pass time I bundled myself up and went for a walk.
Instead of turning towards the main road, which was my
first inclination, I headed the other way, and followed a side
road I hadn't been down in years. I'd remembered the side
road as a crescent that met up with the main road, but it
turned out I was wrong. The lamps became sparser, the
houses grew smaller, and the street curled into a cul-de-
sac, surrounded by woods. I hesitated, then kept going.
The trees were dispersed in such a way that I could pass
between the trunks, but only by contorting myself. The
ground was covered in thick and gnarled roots. Between

some of the roots were semi-frozen puddles, and when I tapped the surface with the soles of my boots the layer of ice cracked into shards and sank into the marshy liquid beneath. The farther in I went, the darker and thicker the woods grew. Just as I was wondering whether I should, or even could, find my way back, I heard cars gliding over asphalt. Headlights sliced through the branches. A few more steps and I was standing on the side of the main road. Two minutes from my street.

Back at my house I checked with my parents, to see if I'd missed any calls, then went to my room and pulled out my record collection. The first record I picked was the Hungarian Dances, conducted by Toscanini. After going through all twenty-one, I replayed the fifth a few more times. Next I listened to *Pini di Roma* and *Fontane di Roma*. Moving from full orchestra to solo instrumentalist, I put on the Casals version of Bach's capacious Cello Suites. I listened to Liszt's teardrop "Consolations," as performed by Rubinstein. After that I went to Chopin's preludes, also Rubinstein's recording. I listened to Walter Gieseking's Bergamasque Suite against Van Cliburn's version. It had been years since I'd played some of these records, but they sounded exactly as I remembered. I knew each performer's idiosyncrasies, statements, hesitations. The moments of counterintuitive boldness that were the marks of personality. I must have listened to over four hours of music, because by the time I got to bed it was well after midnight.

❖

On Christmas morning I was woken twice. At seven I
heard the garage door open, a motor start, and tires crunch
down the driveway. I fell back to sleep. At ten o'clock it was
a clash of baking trays, the buzz of an oven timer, and my
mother knocking on my bedroom door.

"Yes?" I said.

She opened it a crack, letting in the buttery smell of
rising pie crust. "Heading off shortly. Sure you won't come?"

I rubbed my eyes and sat up in bed. "Thanks, but I'd
probably be leaving halfway through for Dirk's, so I'd
prefer not."

"Always welcome if you change your mind."

When I heard the front door close I got out of bed and,
through the bedroom window, watched my mother cross
the street holding a foil-covered ceramic tray. It had snowed
through the night. Light, dry snow. It was piled up on bare
branches, eavestroughs, mailboxes, doorsteps, curbs, side-
view mirrors, windshields, and bumpers. The lawns and
roads were transformed into woolly white carpets.

I couldn't just wait in bed, so I got up and walked
around the house, tapping my fingers along the counters,
cupboards, fridge door, the lid of the piano. At noon, I went
back upstairs, stripped off my pyjamas, and rinsed myself in
the shower. I thought of putting together a lunch from last
night's leftovers but ate a bowl of cereal instead. The next
time I looked at the clock it was half past one. I figured I
had a couple hours to kill. If I didn't hear from Dirk by three
thirty, I would call him, to see if everything was all right.

In the meantime, I did the usual thing. Practise. Schubert and Rachmaninoff and back to the top. Again and again or I'd never make it to Carnegie Hall. Around three o'clock, it began to snow again. Fat flakes, singles and pairs that rotated on shared axes, bedding lightly on the ground. The next time I looked it was a solid curtain, opening and closing in a mesmerizing whiteout.

Three thirty. Four o'clock. Four fifteen. I was anxious. I wondered if something had happened to his flight. A delay or cancellation, a missed connection? Something on the drive home from Schiphol?

I inhaled and exhaled. Just call, Jan.

*Just call.*

The phone in the kitchen started ringing. I let it ring three times before picking it up. I cleared my throat.

"Jan speaking," I said.

"Dirk speaking," he said, deadpan.

"Motherfucker," I said, feeling a flush of relief. "You left it late."

Dirk ignored this. Without prompting, he unleashed a monologue about the last four months. Classes, the campus at large, trips to the city, all the friends he was making, his roommate from California, Drew. Everything going swimmingly.

"That's good," I said. "Really. I'm glad I could get all this information in one handy package, but have you saved me any truffles?"

"Whoa, whoa, Old Man in a hurry. What about you? What's up with you?"

Everything he told me, I repeated back to him in some way. How I had made a few friends myself, what their names were, how a few of us were planning our own trip to some city, which was an idea that someone had floated and nobody had followed up on.

"That's good, Jan," he said. "That's good."

For a second the line went quiet. I felt he was going to say something, but he didn't.

"Dirk?"

"Yes?"

"So what time should I come over?"

Again the line went quiet. I heard voices on Dirk's end. "Is that the fam?" I said.

"No," Dirk said. "My parents are on vacation this year. Belize. Apparently my mother had always wanted to go."

"So if they're not in Den Bosch . . ."

"Neither am I."

"No?" I frowned. I wasn't getting it.

"No, I'm calling from my girlfriend's, Donna's, fam. The Koches."

I took a second.

"Are the Koches like the Zoetmulders, Dirk? Are you at the Zoetmulders'? If you are I can probably see you through the window."

"No," Dirk said. "I'm at the Koches'. In Annapolis, Maryland, the U.S.A."

"You're serious?" I said, unable to stop myself. Obviously Dirk was serious. He'd been serious from our hellos.

"Yeah," he said. "Sorry I didn't call earlier."

"Well," I said, trying to recover, "it's no problem. It's pretty hectic being home, actually. I've barely had time to see my parents with all this work and practising to get through, so . . ."

"That's good," Dirk said. "Good to be busy."

"Yeah, absolutely."

Another drop in the line. I heard raised voices on his end, a harsh dissonance, followed by a group of people laughing.

"Okay," he said.

"Right," I said. "So, are you coming back this break at all?"

"Well, actually, my parents will be coming to see me after New Year's. We'll be spending a few days in New York City to round things off."

"Wow," I said. "Amazing."

"Yeah. I haven't told my parents but Donna's probably going to come along."

Dirk's hand muffled the receiver. Then he was back.

"Yeah, anyways, this is long distance, so . . ."

"Right. Of course. Can I give you a ring this term?"

"At my dorm?"

He recited the digits. I wrote them down.

"Cool, great. Merry Christmas, Jan."

"You too, Dirk."

He hung up. I listened to the dial tone for a while, then hung up too. I walked back to the living room, hunched onto the sofa, and for what seemed like ages I did not move. I held my head in my hands. I felt my stomach turn. "Donna." "Annapolis." "New York City." I didn't believe it. Couldn't believe it. But what did it matter what I believed?

I became furious. Furious at Dirk, but more at myself. I had been weak on the phone. Pathetic. I thought of calling him back. I wanted to call him back. But what would I say?

I stood up. Still not thinking, not feeling, I headed to the piano, squeezing my hands into fists then stretching my fingers backwards, till they hurt.

I started with the Rachmaninoff, the piece Dirk would have liked. I went straight to my favourite section, the tumbling four-note chords, and played it repeatedly. Each time I inverted the tempo a little, so largo was eventually played presto and vice versa. I moved to the Schubert, where I changed the major chords to minor and made suspended seconds into sharp sevenths, turning the piece's hesitations and expectations into ugliness and violence. Where I read pianissimo, I played forte. Staccato passages were suppressed by the damper pedal. Brightness smothered at the bottom of a black well.

When I stopped playing I put my hands to my ears and listened as a circle of music formed around my head. I listened to this circle as if it were a recording. When the recording ended, I went back to playing, this time louder, more aggressively. I pressed my hands to my ears to test the playback. I played again, longer, louder, and kept testing. I wanted to make a recording that would go on indefinitely, to create a fortress of sound. Whatever it took, I would do it. Outside it was dark. I was still alone. I went back to playing. Held the pedal longer. Played louder. When I paused, I put my hands to my ears. Listened. And started again.

For years after that Christmas I did not once speak to Dirk or hear from him, nor did he hear from me. I turned to other things. Music. I had his number and could have tracked him through his college, but he could have done the same for me.

At the end of my first year at de Groot I looked at what I had done. I was on partial scholarship, meant to be a promising talent, and yet had accomplished nothing since leaving Sint Ansfried except build a repertoire of a few dozen pieces. I had yet to understand music as something beyond a pattern of notes on a grid, or to conceive of a piece as a story, and of composers as storytellers with specific voices, cadences, personalities. I had yet to see that a composition could be an anecdote or comedy or epic, or that you could communicate a piece of music to an audience like the two of you were sitting at a café table, and that all the gesticulations, pauses, and outpourings of sweat that are part of the telling could be included in a performance.

After first year I decided that, while I could not make up for the past, I could make the best of what was still ahead. I spent the summer in Maastricht, practising and practising, speeding up and covering more ground. I started dreaming again, about playing with a quintet in Leipzig, recording a studio album with EMI, attending a masterclass with Colin Davis in Birmingham. All things that would impress Dirk, even if he didn't know who Colin Davis was.

The practice rooms at the faculty were open twenty-four hours a day and I regularly practised until the early hours of the morning. As soon as I woke up the next day, I started again. I became more clever about how I used my time. I tape-recorded my sessions, met outside class hours with a tutor, and read and researched composers, as opposed to merely staring at their note-filled pages and wondering how this or that famous pianist, Rubinstein or Richter, would play it.

Twelve months on, at the end of my second year, I looked down at my hands while they played the keyboard and saw, for the first time, the tools of a professional. Precise, controlled, fast, delicate. It was like the sound I was producing came from somewhere beyond the combination of my fingers and the piano. It was like the sound that came from the speakers of my stereo. The sound of a concert pianist playing to a sold-out five-thousand-seat auditorium.

In my third year I went from middle of the pack, a competent but easily overlooked student, to head of the class. I won the Sweelinck Scholarship, the school's premier prize, and performed in solo and group recitals at the faculty and in public. I also focused my repertoire. Chopin, Ravel, Debussy, Fauré, Saint-Saëns, Satie. Nineteenth- and early twentieth-century composers, mostly French.

By now, the music never left me. I no longer had to cover my ears to test if it was still there. The music I played during the day was the last thing I heard before I went to sleep, and the first thing I heard when I woke up.

And outside the room, I got on with life too. I went on my own to London and Paris. Bought clothes without a second thought, and even developed a sense of style. I went out to bars and, once or twice, to restaurants. I went to parties and met girls who knew nothing about me but what they saw. I went down on a girl for the first time. I tried dating. I had a few steadies, though nothing serious. I acted aloof to see what it felt like. I liked being distant, unreceptive, a little mysterious, as if I'd always been head of the class, and I did not talk much about my life before Maastricht.

Then I met Lena.

In August, one week before the start of my final year, the class tutor, Arne, told me I'd been chosen for a solo performance at the conservatory's annual showcase concert, which was staged for booking agents, professional musicians, and company managers from across Europe. Even though there was a glut of awards for graduating students, the showcase was the biggest of the big deals. When word got around, a couple of classmates organized a small celebration.

Deciding it would be low-key, we headed to our local, across from the Onze Lieve Vrouwe church. Tables were set outside, in the square, but those were for the tourists, and we went inside, to the usual cloud of cigarette smoke, blaring music, and roster of self-involved bartenders. We were on our way to a table in the far corner when I saw a girl, although really she was more a woman, sitting on a bar stool. Perched, with perfect posture and a long neck. She had a round face, a small, sharp chin, dark eyes, and was wearing a thin sweater that clung to her breasts and waist. When she turned to grab the bartender's attention, I saw she had golden-blond hair, and that it reached down to the small of her back.

In that instant, my classmates disappeared, the noise in the bar quieted to drifts of sound, and I was struck by a need for this girl who was a woman. Unlike anything I'd felt before. It hurt not to have her already.

I don't know who that person was who walked up to the bar without a single intelligent thought in his head, or who sat on the stool beside her and smiled, or who was going to get the bartender's attention just to have something to say. I don't know where I found the guts to be that person, maybe it was from the news Arne had just given me, but there I was. I raised my hand, about to call out an order to the bartender who had his back to us, and this girl, who had barely lifted an eyebrow when I smiled at her, said, "The good ones have radar." She cleared her throat and the bartender instantly spun around to take her order.

"And what'll your friend have?" the bartender asked.

I don't know what I ordered. Whatever she was having? A beer? What mattered is I introduced myself, we started talking, she gave me her number, and when I called it, two days later, she answered. We spoke and, as casually as I could, I asked her on a date.

The very second she said yes, as if it was the obvious answer to the question, I started to sweat. What to wear? What to say? How to act?

But like at the bar, Lena took care of everything. She chose the place to meet and, afterwards, the place to eat. The restaurant was an out-of-the-way Thai or Indonesian or, in any case, Asian place. Lena ordered because nothing on the menu was familiar to me. I don't remember what we talked about, but all the words came with ease. What I do remember is picking up, and imprinting in my memory, the details I didn't see the first time. The unblemished white around her dark irises. The dimple above her top lip and shadow of another dimple on her chin. The part on the left side of her head and the hair that swooped across her brow. Her almost swollen lips, which I wanted to feel on mine every time she smiled.

The only lighting in the room came from a wick sunken in a fortress of wax, and in that flickering light, Lena frequently touched her face with her hands when she spoke. She said later that she knew her hands, especially her long fingers, were her most beautiful body part and she had deliberately touched her face as often as possible throughout the dinner.

After the restaurant we went to a bar, then we walked towards her apartment, which she told me was across the river in one of the low-rises near the old ceramic factories. There was an early-fall chill. She placed my arm over her shoulder and smiled. I thought I was going to go home with her but at the bridge she said goodnight and embraced me. No opportunity for a kiss. She just walked away. And as with everything that night, she knew exactly what she was doing because right up till the next time I saw her I was burning to kiss her. And determined to never let her walk away from me again.

Lena killed Lise. She killed Stefa at the height of Stefa, not to mention wiping the floor with Horseface, Beate, and anyone else from my afternoon fantasies. Nobody in my past had a stitch on Lena, and the thought of these comparisons, which popped up at the beginning, made me, for the first time in ages, want to somehow contact my old best friend and send him a photograph of my new girlfriend with a note that said, "See?"

But that would have been a short sell, and I knew right away something greater was happening. In what seemed like no time, it was Lena who came to sit invisibly in my classes; Lena to whom I told my stories at the end of the day. I started staying overnight at her apartment, and within a couple of weeks I stored toiletries in her bathroom and a change of clothes in her drawers.

Lena's place was on the third floor of her building. Through her bedroom window you had a clear view of the Maas and of the old city, which had been my world for the last three years. Sometimes, at the end of the day, I'd stand by the window and look at the sun set over the broadening river, and it was like being on the deck of a boat that was sailing away from a harbour, with the dots moving along the far bank being the crowd seeing me off. As the shadows cut in, the old city would disappear, part by part. Steeples, gabled roofs, street corners, alleyways, riverbanks. Soon after would come the jangle of keys telling me Lena was home.

When we met, Lena, who was two years older than me, was doing her legal apprenticeship with a firm called Herm Frisch. She started work at nine, came home at seven, showered daily, dressed like an adult, collected a cheque once a month. Real life. And she made it clear that if I wanted to spend time with her while she was awake, I'd have to change my daily schedule. So I did. Instead of heading out to the practice rooms mid-afternoon and staying till past midnight, I began early in the day and ended around the time Lena clocked off. I had a proper breakfast before leaving and took a lunch with me, so I wasn't spending money at the student café. I was becoming domesticated, and I liked it. I liked showing Lena I could accommodate.

But as late October arrived, and the date of the showcase concert approached, I had to go back to the old ways. When

Lena saw the hours I spent in the practice rooms, she said it was her turn to adjust, and more often than not, she'd come with me, bringing office work with her. On the way to the rooms, I'd put my arm around her shoulder or she'd run her fingers through my hair, and we'd daydream about what it would be like after the showcase. After graduation. She took it as a given I'd be on tour and she'd be with me.

"I want to go to America first," she'd say.

"America? First?"

"I've never been," she said.

"Neither have I."

"I'm thinking New York," she'd say a little later. "Driving down Broadway."

I might have added something about a stretch limo with an open sunroof, but didn't doubt her vision. She spoke about us in terms of years and sometimes even decades, and very quickly, as if I'd been waiting for them without knowing it, these visions worked their way inside me. Marriage. Anniversary parties surrounded by friends we'd yet to make. Famous occasions where we'd meet other musicians, travel to exotic places, cross all the oceans.

Then I'd go into the practice room and she'd sit down by the door, spreading her work around her. It was torture to turn away from her, but I didn't have to wait for the spark to take over—I had fear working as well. The showcase was coming. The days were flying by and I still had the earth to do. I took out my notebook and music, set specific goals for the session, and got started.

At least once an hour, though, I'd slip off the bench and look out the door at a napping Lena, leaning against the doorframe with head back, lips parted, eyes closed. When I looked at her in these moments I was overcome. The music I had been practising went on playing in my head, but as background.

As softly as possible, I'd walk out and kiss her shadow-dimpled chin, her cheek, her ear. With eyes still closed she'd smile. She did that, smiling when she was neither awake nor asleep. Sometimes she even answered questions, or ran her fingers through my hair. Then the smile would fade, the lips close, and the arm fall slowly to her side. I'd whisper to her about her face or her fingers or her hair to see if I'd get a reaction.

I was performing Schubert's Sonata in B-flat for the showcase; originally Arne's idea. He'd overheard me playing it one day and convinced me I had a connection to this piece that I hadn't shown in others. Now, he said, the job was to reinvent the sonata, bar by bar, note by note. An enormous undertaking, and I don't know how I would have got on with it if Lena had not been there every day, a reminder that I was no longer on my own. She used to joke that when I didn't want to run an errand or complete a tedious task, I should think of doing it "for us." Soon it became part of our normal conversation. Leave work on time for us. Eat this last bit of leftovers for us. When I left Lena with a kiss and went back to the practice room, it was for us.

❖

The de Groot Conservatory's thirty-seventh annual show-case took place on a Thursday in late November, exactly two weeks before my twenty-third birthday. The faculty's music hall, where the performance would take place, was a room with three hundred and fifty grey felt-covered seats arranged on a slope towards a semi-circular stage. Above the stage was a frescoed half-dome, which hid a bank of stage lights. On either side were heavy curtains brocaded in a modern geometric style.

On the final day of rehearsal I came early, while the conservatory orchestra was finishing a run-through of *Die Moldau*. To pass time, I sat in the back row and picked out classmates onstage. All were staring intently at their scores, only occasionally breaking their concentration to glance at the conductor. Like drivers checking their mirrors.

As the rehearsal went on, though, I stopped paying close attention and instead mentally cleared the players offstage. In place of their chairs, stands, sheet music, and percussion instruments, I put a solitary Steinway, a Hamburg D. The high altar of concert pianos. In my imagination, I dimmed the house lights and raised the stage lights. Through a thin opening at stage right, I had a pianist walk out from the wings. That pianist was me. He sat on the Hamburg D's bench, adjusted the height, and straightened his back. Like everyone else in the audience I was watching the pianist closely, waiting for that first note. And in that moment of expectation, as the pianist was lifting his arms and leaning towards the keyboard,

my mind flashed to a memory of Dirk: the first time he'd
come to one of my shows. It was a "Young Musicians"
performance held at Vlijmen town hall. He'd been making
fun for weeks leading up to it. "Do you want me to wear
my culottes? What do we say when we are greeted by the
king? When the harp plays, do we automatically cry? What
do you mean, there's not going to be a harp?" When I
tried to remind him about the time and place on the day
of the recital to make sure he'd be there, he just repeated
"M'lady m'lady m'lady" again and again. On the night of
the performance, when I looked over the audience, I saw
Dirk sitting in the middle, halfway back, looking unusu-
ally reserved. The stage lights went up. I played my piece.
And when it ended, I again looked over the audience and
saw everyone politely applauding except for Dirk, who
was standing on his chair, hooting, waving, pumping his
fists, utterly monkey.

The surging and wind-tossed strings in the final section of *Die Moldau* shook me back to the present. Arne
had slipped into the hall while I wasn't paying attention
and sat down next to me. I nodded at him. On the stage,
the conductor squeezed the fingers of his right hand,
making an end to the piece. Arne applauded, ostensibly
congratulating the orchestra but also, it seemed, to usher
them offstage. He turned to me.

"Come on," he said, "work to do."

We stepped down to the stage, where the chairs and
stands were being carried off to make way for the piano.

As I ran over the piece with Arne that afternoon, work went on all around. Lights were adjusted. Curtains tested. I could see, through the open door at the back of the auditorium, the staff filling the ticket office lightbox with headshots of the principal performers, including myself, and raised plastic letters announcing the program. Bedřich Smetana, *Die Moldau*. M. O. Pallett, Cloud Cycle. Intermission. Franz Schubert, Sonata in B-flat, *performed by Jan de Vries*.

As I finished up, someone on the crew was testing the bulb in the lightbox, flashing it on and off. Lightbox on, lightbox off. On. Off. On, staying on. Jan de Vries. Fat.

On the morning of the concert, Lena reminded me she wouldn't see me till after the performance, and asked if I was sure I knew what I was wearing, where the shoe polish was stored, which necktie to choose. I told her I had no idea where any of these things was but I would be fine.

She left happy, and I spent the rest of the morning padding around the apartment looking for ways to kill time, or bypass it, as the suspense of the performance was building. As morning was turning to afternoon I noticed that, as I listened to passages of the sonata in my head, playing out as I had practised them these past several weeks, I was also catching scraps of an alternate version, and that it sounded the way I'd played it years ago, in my empty house on Christmas Day. It was as if the alternate version were trying to insinuate itself into the ideal one. Several times I "restarted" the piece the correct way, but each time the other, strange way would edge in. As an experiment, I decided to let the sonata play out, and when it did I found the correct version would take over. I wasn't worried by the confusion, but when it was resolved I felt relief, even a bit of happiness; the two versions could cooperate. Like two plots joining into a storyline.

At six thirty I arrived at the backstage entrance to the faculty music hall and went down to the green room. As it got close to seven, I listened to the bustle of the arriving crowd. I imagined seats filling up, the audience members chatting, and somewhere in the wings the musicians nervously waiting for the chance to strike their first notes. Downstairs, I was fidgeting just the same. First with the clothes I was wearing, then with a particularly interesting light switch, then with my own fingers and fingernails. I thought of Glenn Gould's pre-performance habits: humming, dancing, bathing his fingers in a basin of warm water. His late-career compulsions, like wearing non-prescription glasses onstage and setting up with a score he didn't actually use. Before I knew it, I could hear the Cloud Cycle coming to an end. I listened to the applause, the footsteps of a moving herd. Intermission. Stands and chairs being scraped across the boards, a piano being rolled into position.

On cue, a knock on the door: the ten-minute warning. I looked at the small mirror on the back of the green room's door, unbuttoned and rebuttoned my collar, checked my fly, retied my shoelaces. Another knock: five minutes. I walked up to the wings, hoping not to pass anyone I knew so as not to have to speak. On stage, two men were making the final adjustments to the concert grand. Arne was wiping the lacquered black rim with a white cloth to remove the fingerprints. As they worked on raising the lid I checked the clock backstage. At three minutes to go, beneath the sound of ushers shimmering their chimes to tell people to take their seats, I began to hear in my head the first bars of the first movement. Arne had given me advice for just this moment.

"Don't worry about the little things," he said. "I'll be there to check the bench is at the right height, the stand is down, the lid at the angle you like. In the last minutes, as you wait in the wings and the audience finds their seats, you may notice a static of expectation. The air will get thicker. Take it in. Use it as a kind of armour."

Arne was right; the air felt denser, and the music stands, instrument cases, stacks of chairs, and every other object around me seemed heavier, bigger, more consequential. I looked past the curtains. The last of the audience were taking their seats. First-year students. Members of faculty. A few young men, thin and bespectacled and wearing sharp suits with notepads in hand, probably agency reps. I looked down to the front row, to Lena. Her recently cut hair was angled sharply just below the ears. Her gold hoop earrings, which I especially liked, dangled just below the cut. Wine-dark lipstick stained her already full lips.

With the audience in their seats, the house lights dimmed and the stage lights bloomed inside their black metal frames. It was time. Inside my head the opening bars of the first movement grew louder, almost raucous. A crowd waiting for the show to start. My palms were sweating and a buzz ran through my fingers.

Here was the moment I had worked for. I thought of all the hours I'd spent at the Grotrian, in my parents' living room, on my own. Not paying attention to the weather outside, or what people were doing in it. Not caring about anything but the bar, line, piece I was practising, again and again. From the solitude of practising I had come to the cusp of appearing before an audience. An audience waiting to hear me. And now I had the chance to make this the first of hundreds, thousands, such shows.

I walked onstage and sat on the bench. A brief applause, then quiet. I placed my hands in position on either side of middle C. One-five-one B-flat octave in the right hand. Root position B-flat triad in the left. Light but steady on the eighth notes, I said to myself. Mind leaving the foot too long on the pedal. Don't let up on the staccato in the left-hand intervals. I breathed out, held it, and pressed from the shoulders. My fingers, once they fell into rhythm, played on their own. In my mind, I was on a bicycle, picking up speed. The wind cut through my hair, skimmed my sides, shook the nearby branches; it bent the long grass over the dykes and rippled the surface of the canal. I stood on my pedals and could hear every note in the rush of air. When one movement ended, I started right into the next, before the audience had the chance to exhale. Keeping them on the edge of their seats, playing counter to their expectations, that was the idea. Whatever version of the Schubert they came in knowing by heart, automatically humming when they heard the words "Sonata in B-flat," I wanted to make sure they left with my version in their ears, unable to think it was ever played otherwise.

As the fourth movement, which double-knotted the laces from previous sections, reached the end, I slowed the bounce of the major chords, leaving an eerie pause between some, as if second-guessing them. Entering the last lines, I opened my eyes, just for a moment, to set my hands for the final tumble of notes. Then I squeezed them shut again, threw my head back, let my hands find their own way, and cut the final note short. My last move was to hold my hands a foot above the keys, fingers spread, as though music was still emanating from the instrument. I wanted everyone to hear, like I did, the afterlife of the piece.

The applause came like a speeding train, and like a person standing too close to the edge of a platform, I was physically brushed back. So much work, so many hours, and I had arrived. As I stood to take my bows, the clapping turned rhythmic, with a few hoots thrown in, and I remembered despite myself Dirk, ballistically pumping his fists in the air. After leaving the stage I went back for an encore, buzzing through a jangling, blustery version

of Rachmaninoff's C-sharp prelude. Limbs falling spectacularly down stairs.

With the last of the piece's power chords I left the stage
under a fresh hail of hooting and clapping. The first person
I saw backstage was Arne.

"You've absolutely done it, de Vries. First class. I've
seen plenty take this stage and I'm telling you I wouldn't
be surprised if you signed with an agency tomorrow."

Lena came rushing in behind him and kissed me all
over the face, in front of everyone.

Arne had been exaggerating, but not by much. Within
days, envelopes started filling the dormitory mail slot,
most of them form letters with fresh signatures, but a
few handwritten inquiries on personal letterhead. Could
I come to their offices? Could I call at this number? We
certainly look forward to seeing you. That first week, I
travelled to Amsterdam, Rotterdam, Den Haag. I was
taken to lunches and dinners in downtown restaurants. I
rode the train in first class and was chauffeured by junior
reps from the agencies. "Almost as if I was some kind of
hotshot lawyer," I said to Lena.

One of the agents suggested a tour of America. Another
a series in Germany.

Every day some news came. Everything a cause for Lena
and me to celebrate.

My mind, having taken a hiatus during the last days of
preparation for the showcase, went back to daydreaming

my future with Lena. The two of us living together in our own place. Taking road trips down the Rhine or Danube or Canal du Midi. Lena and me in Rome. In bed reading beside each other. In a fancy restaurant. In a seedy bar. Hiking, even though I didn't like hiking. On a ferry some- where. Playing minigolf on the ferry. Time passing but never getting old. We started saying "I'm going to marry you" to each other. It was as effortless and inevitable as everything else.

After the initial flurry of meetings, I signed papers with Alderdink and Associates. Their reputation was excellent, and a number of the tutors encouraged me. As far as I could tell, there were no real associates. Just Alderdink, a portly, suspenders-wearing, cigarillo-smoking man in his fifties who went by his first name, Taub. As soon as I scribbled my signature on the contracts, Taub revealed he had my first date set up for after graduation, a concert in Osaka. And after that, four performances over three weeks elsewhere in Japan and Korea.

"Ever been to the East, de Vries? Twelve hours on a plane, eh. Better get used to it!"

Taub laughed. Then he handed me a score and laughed some more. It was the sheet music for Debussy's *En Blanc et Noir*, a piece for two pianos. "Hell of a first movement," he said. "But I'm sure you knew that. The crowds want technical fireworks these days, and you're going to deliver."

I went to Lena's apartment right after to tell her the first stop wasn't America, but Japan. She was sheer joy at the news, and right away pulled a beaten *Bosatlas* off her shelf to scan the Asia maps and pick out city names and travel distances.

I stayed at her apartment straight through the following week, culminating in my birthday, number twenty-three, when Lena and I stayed up most of the night to celebrate. Like a boxer who lets himself go after a title fight, I didn't go to the practice rooms once during that time. But I knew eventually I'd have to rouse myself, and the cue was opening the sheet music Taub had given me. The first movement. I'd never performed anything like it, never seen a score like it. But I was at a high point in my confidence. I'd trained for this, was ready for it. I thought of the late nights at the faculty, the addictive adrenaline of a deadline, and could feel the nervous excitement bubbling up inside me.

Two weeks into my mad dash through *En Blanc et Noir*, after an all-nighter in the practice rooms, I stopped by the dorm. I wanted to pick up a few books, references to help with the piece. As I walked into the building half dazed from the long night, dragging my feet along the tiles of the foyer, the porter called something in my direction. My name, though it took a few tries till he caught my attention.

I rubbed my eyes and apologized. The porter handed me a stack of envelopes.

"More offers, de Vries?"

"That ship's sailed," I said with a touch of the arrogance that Lena had recently been warning me against.

I climbed the stairs to my room shuffling through the envelopes, curious to know who else might have written. A few late requests from agents, some whose names I recognized, some I didn't. Campus mail. Something that looked like an invoice, but who knew for what. I was at my door when I got to a sky-blue envelope with a border of navy and red stripes. A sticker pasted to the front said "Air Mail" in English. There were stars and stripes on the stamp. The address was dashed off in almost illegible, but familiar, handwriting. I stopped short, then grabbed my keys, opened the door, and sat on the edge of the bed. I tore one side of the envelope and fished out a folded sheet of waxy thin blue paper.

The calligraphy, appalling as ever. Jumbled words, scratched-out words, the point of the pen threatening everywhere to puncture the page. I smoothed it out one or two times.

Dear dear *dear* de Vries,

 I don't know if you will get this or not but you know what I want to say my dearest sweetest most wonderful wonder of a friend is —

Happy motherfucking birthday to you.
Happy goddamned birthday.
Oh Good Lord, Sweet Jesus of Lazarus,
Happy goddamned motherfucking *birthday*
dear Old Man de Vries . . .

Now go get drunk and watch out for venereal
diseases.

Heaven above, oh heaven above. May your birthday,
day of days, moment of history, pivotal instant in the
universe, be happy. I miss you grandly, goodness gra-
cious me. So many things have happened over here.
Much news to tell, colourful and strange, twenty-four
hours a day. But first, what have you been up to? What
are you doing? Please, please not all at once. Hold
some in reserve. I'll be home in December so fill me
in then. That's right. *Then.* In the meantime, little de
Vries, allow yourself to be left with the following: "*Hi,
everybody. I'm Archie Bell and the Drells, from Houston,
Texas. We don't only sing but we dance just as good as we
want.*"                                                    D.

I shook the envelope. There was something else inside. A
photocopied sheet, folded over like a booklet, fell out. On
the cover was a grainy image of two people, one standing
and one kneeling. The standing person held a sword to
the shoulder of the kneeling person, as if knighting him.
The picture was too rough to tell if either was Dirk. Or
neither. In small writing, beneath the picture, was a title.
*Elsinoreville.* Inside was a list of names. Melissa, Markus,
Drew, Stephen, Dirk.

I dropped the program on the bed and went back to
the letter. It looked like a relic but carried his voice clear as

day. As if he were in front of me. I read it one more time, then folded the paper along its crease and slipped it, and the program, back into the envelope.

I left the letter in my dorm room and went to Lena's, where I put on some music and decided to make filet mignon with asparagus, my one and only specialty.

Three days later, I picked up the phone to call Den Bosch. Though I had stewed over the decision, when I finally dialed the number it felt spontaneous, even liberating. A housekeeper answered, which caught me off guard. I left my dorm number, Lena's number, and the last day I'd be in Maastricht.

That night when Lena came home, I told her I'd gotten a letter from an old friend. "Dirk Noosen," I said. "We were close at Sint Ansfried. Best friends. Then he went to school overseas and kind of fell off the map."

Lena was unpacking her briefcase on the kitchen table and didn't say anything.

"He's coming back and wants to meet up," I said.

Lena looked up. "Exciting, no?"

"Well," I said, "yes. Dirk's a different kind of person. When we were at Sint Ansfried, everyone loved him. He always had the girls. I guess now the table's turned."

"That's your first reaction?"

"We were very competitive," I said, by way of apology.

Lena laughed. "Just teasing." She began to take out plates for dinner. "So when will we be seeing him?"

"Around Christmas," I said. Lena nodded. She didn't ask further about Dirk, didn't even say more about the idea of being paraded like a trophy in front of him.

As the end of term approached, I started anticipating a call or note from Dirk. I went about my routine as normal, meeting with Arne, polishing an essay for my theory course, but I kept an eye on the phone in Lena's apartment, and when I slept there I'd drop by the dormitory the next morning to see if he'd left a message. On December twenty-third, Lena and I were due at her parents' house, where I'd meet her family for the first time and spend Christmas and New Year's. I had told that to the housekeeper, so if Dirk got the message, he would know the date. With less than a week left, the rational part of me was reconciled to the likelihood Dirk wouldn't show up, but the irrational part, which was stronger, was almost certain he would.

On the eve of our departure Lena and I were in my dorm room, packing. It was going slowly, Lena taking every opportunity to look through my belongings, including a duffle bag of old clothes and a shoebox of notes and photos I'd brought from Vlijmen, which I hadn't looked through in years.

"When did you last wear these?" Lena asked. "Who's the girl in this picture? You *liked* this band?"

It was all a joke to her, especially because she saw I was sensitive. "Which pictures should I bring to show my family? How about this one? They'll be thrilled to know I'm dating someone who was still playing with plastic swords as a teenager." While I was swatting her comments away, the telephone rang. Lena was closer and picked it up.

"Hello?" she said. "Mm-hm. No, I'm not. Yes, he is. One second, please." She handed me the receiver.

"Hello?"

It was the porter's desk. "There's a gentleman here to see you, de Vries."

A gentleman.

"He says"—a hand covered the receiver—"his name's Frank Herbert."

"I'll be down in a sec," I said, hanging up the phone and throwing the folded shirts on the bed. "We'll do this later," I said to Lena. "It's Dirk."

"Who?"

"Dirk, my old friend. He's downstairs."

"You didn't say he was coming today. What about all this?" She waved towards the clothes on the bed, the open suitcase.

"C'mon," I said, "we'll finish later. Promise."

Lena nodded, skeptically, and got up. I hustled us out of the room. I could feel jitters in my knees. Half a flight down and Lena was already three steps behind. "Come on!"

As I turned the corner into the foyer I could hear his voice. The husky edge always on the verge of making a crude joke.

"Yeah, everything in America's different. *Especially . . .*"

I stopped. Looked. Dirk was leaning against the front desk, talking to the porter like they were old pals. One foot crossed over the other, an arm spread over the counter, fingers fidgeting with the corner of the sign-in sheet. Hair a mess. Ears red from the cold.

"Frank?" I called out.

He turned. Round, smiling eyes. Chip on the front tooth. "I thought you'd like that one," he said.

We walked to each other. I reached out an arm, as if to shake his hand, but it got lost as he pulled me in for a hug.

"Old Man, Old Man."

Dirk laughed. He squeezed his arms around me. I smiled.

When Lena cleared her throat behind me, Dirk let go and I turned around. "This is Lena. My, *ahem*, serious girlfriend." I slipped my arm around her waist. "Lena, this is Dirk. Dirk Noosen."

Dirk leaned back and looked Lena up and down. She blushed.

"Hope I'm not interrupting," Dirk said.

"We were on the verge of leaving town," I said. "A heads-up would've been nice!"

Lena broke in. "Are you here for the night, Dirk, or are you staying longer?"

"A couple of days," he said, clapping his hands together. "I'm with a friend of my father's, on the north end of town. I think it's north. Never been here before."

"We could go out for a coffee right now," I said.

Dirk nodded.

I looked at Lena. "The Easy?" I asked.

"Okay," she said. She must have been thinking of all that was left to do upstairs, but she was being a good sport about it. "I'll run up and get our coats."

The Easy, that night, was full. Dirk and I got a four-seater near the front window. Lena went to look at the choice of pastries and order for us. Dirk watched as she squeezed between tables. "Tight jeans," he said as she passed from earshot. "Tight jeans ordering your dessert."

He looked around the room and bobbed his head. We were, for the moment, alone. The strangeness of it, Dirk's instant immediacy after such a long absence. I had envisioned this. Imagined my possible responses. Haughty. Passive-aggressive. Just plain aggressive. But now he was here, in front me, I felt myself slipping into my old role. I wanted to ask him questions just to hear the answers, stories about where he'd been, his many exploits, true, exaggerated, imaginary. I wanted to wring everything from him at once. To talk about that Christmas, even. Why not? But it was Dirk, as usual, who took the initiative.

Did I remember the time we went to a bar in Den Bosch, like this one, and saw a guy drunk out of his mind rubbing himself against a nut dispensing machine, yelling, *Look at me! I'm fucking nuts!* Did I remember how, later that night, the same man was kissing the nut machine, as if he was trying to make up with it? Did I remember the year we had a vice-principal named Bent? The year we had a supply teacher named Chisholm? That time he went on a date with Sisi Vermeulen and ended up getting sick in one of her gloves?

When Lena came back with cakes and coffees, Dirk distributed the plates and mugs, then added two shots of cream and a mountain of sugar to his and raised it for a toast. "To . . . Ile de Réunion!"

He took a slug that left some liquid dribbling down his chin. He winked at Lena, as if the entire thing were on purpose. She smiled at me. I felt the table warm up.

"Sorry about all that," Dirk said, dabbing at his chin, perhaps sensitive to the idea that he might be crossing a line with Lena. "It's been a while since I saw the Old Man. The silliness stops now. Scout's honour."

After a pause, Lena began to ask Dirk questions. She asked him about school. Living in the United States. Being far from home. His answers were general, his sentences brief. At a certain point he pulled out a pen and started doodling on a napkin, then scratched out what he'd drawn, and crumpled the paper. "Never mind me," he said. "What about you? You two? How long have you been going out?"

I looked over at Lena. "We met at a bar, not far from here." I was trying to control the edge of overconfidence in my voice, but failing. "I saw her, the crowd parted, and that was that."

"Impress, Old Man. Impress. And when did this biblical event take place?"

"Late August," I said, again looking at Lena.

"Seems like longer," she said. "In a good way."

"When's the engagement?" Dirk asked.

"After Lena completes her legal training. Which gives you about six months to steal her away from me."

Dirk smiled and rapped his knuckles across the tabletop. "Still not over that one, eh?"

Lena looked confused; I told her I'd explain later.

"And what about school, de Vries?"

I told him about the Sweelinck prize, the showcase concert, signing with an agent, drawing out certain details, but again unable to help myself, sometimes with Lena egging me on. "I'll be going on tour right after I graduate."

That's when Lena asked Dirk if I'd told him about Japan.

Dirk cocked an eyebrow. "What about Japan?"

Lena looked at me as though she couldn't believe I hadn't said anything. "We," she said, "or at the moment *he*, is going to Osaka in late April to begin his first tour."

Dirk leaned forward. "When were you going to drop that bomb, Old Man?"

"I told you I was going on tour," I said.

He opened his mouth, seemingly on the verge of saying something, then sat back and shook his head. The look on his face said he was doing some kind of mental calculation but couldn't believe the outcome.

"But you didn't say you were going to *Japan*. And in April, of all months."

He was quiet but the wheels were still spinning. Lena and I waited for his next words. Finally he muttered, "I knew there was a reason."

He shifted in his chair. Placed both hands on the table.

"Jan, do you remember . . . *Gargantua*?"

"Of course," I said. I turned to Lena. "It was this play Dirk did about medieval France, based on a sixteenth-century novel."

"Giants, havoc, a character named Dingdong. Actually," Dirk said, "the Old Man here was integral. He thought of performing the music onstage. The big number was some kind of a berserka, right?"

"*Mazurka*. By Chopin."

"Like I said." He paused again. A twinkle in his eye. "What if I were to tell you I'm in the middle of forming a troupe to put on *Gargantua*. Like, right *now*. I've already booked small stages in Chicago and Upstate New York." He looked around, as if checking if someone was overhearing. "And the idea is to bring it to *Japan*. One of the actors found some New Theatre festival in Tokyo, and everyone's super excited about it."

I shook my head. I didn't understand the connection.

He looked around again. "The festival's in *April*! You, me, *Gargantua*, old times, Empire of the Rising Sun!"

"What?"

"Use your eyes to follow my finger, Old Man. We would meet up for your concert in Osaka. Then you two could come to Tokyo for the show."

I started laughing. "Are you serious?"

"You said late April, right?"

"The twenty-first," Lena said. "In Osaka."

Dirk bit his lip and started bouncing in his seat. "I'm thinking we're going to do this. In fact, we are *definitely* going to do this. Dammit," he said, standing up, "this calls for bubbles! Do they serve bubbles here?"

Underneath the table Lena squeezed my wrist.

"Um . . ."

Dirk bolted to the bar. I turned immediately to Lena. "I know. The packing."

"Listen," she said, taking my hands in hers. "I've had a thought. This is fun for you, right? How often do you get to see old friends? I want you to stay."

"What about getting ready?"

"Stay tonight and, if you want, stay for a couple of days. Celebrate everything you've accomplished this term."

"But our plans."

"Don't worry about that. I wouldn't mind a few days on my own to relax. Warm up my parents to the idea that I'm dating an artist. I'll make everything nice and cozy for your arrival. Then you'll come on Christmas Eve, which is the important thing."

"Are you sure?"

Dirk came back to the table, balancing three beers. Lena took the coat off the back of her chair and picked up her purse from under the table.

"Are you leaving because all I got was beer?" Dirk asked.

"It was nice to meet you," Lena said, extending her hand. Dirk took it, pulled her close, and kissed her on both cheeks. Lena laughed, kissing him in return. I pushed back my chair.

"You're not leaving too?" Dirk said.

"I'm going to walk Lena to the door," I said.

Outside, I told Lena I would come back to the dorm that moment, if that's what she wanted.

"The plan's made," she said. "You've been working so hard. Have some fun with your friend." She smiled. "Even if I find him a bit much."

I pressed my lips to hers. "I love you so much," I said.

"I love you too, Jan."

As soon as she turned the corner, I spun back into the Easy. In my absence, Dirk had caught the attention of one of the waiters and asked for a menu.

"Think we need a second round of these beers, no? And probably a couple shots. Good for making complicated plans."

Over the next two days, Dirk and I went everywhere in Maastricht. I took my bike out of the dorm's storage and Dirk rode Lena's, having promised to be careful with it.

The first day, I showed him around my new city. Riverside, cafés, my favourite second-hand record store. We ate dinner standing up in a kebab shop and had some beers in a bar across the way. Heading back to the dorm, we passed a club that blared music onto the street, and Dirk, with a dangerous look in his eyes, persuaded me to go in, and pay our cover. We spent the night dancing, with Dirk pointing out women who either ignored him or gave him eyes, and in the early hours stumbled back to the dorm, where Dirk crashed on the couch, snoring so loudly it was hard for me to get to sleep.

The next day, the plan had been to show Dirk around de Groot but we woke up late, with hangovers, and Dirk proposed instead that we take a train to the nearest Belgian town to buy some pot. I argued with him all the way to the station, where Dirk bought two tickets on the Ostend local. We got off a half-hour later in a small town, and Dirk, as if following some inner compass, led the way to the main road, where we found a kid in a beat-up denim jacket pacing the pavement.

"I've never done this before," I said.

"Well, I've never been to this town before," said Dirk, "so technically neither have I."

I picked a coin out of my pocket. "Loser buys," I said, but Dirk caught the coin in mid-air.

"Remember when we flipped on *Caligula?*" he said. The previews made the entire movie look like one long orgy scene; sheer salivation at the prospect of seeing it. When it came time to buy tickets, we flipped a coin. I lost, but Dirk, sensing my mortification was too great to overcome, went to the counter by himself and paid. Now he pocketed my coin as tribute, approached the kid on the walk, and five minutes later we were crouching behind a building while

Dirk rolled joints with some paper he had on him. He lit two and passed one to me; we split a third on the train back to Maastricht; a fourth as we walked out the station and along the Maas.

It was close to the end of the day when Dirk went back to the subject of Japan.

"*Oishi-katta*. That's Japanese for 'berserka.' Or, wait, I mean 'delicious.' See? I've been studying."

"Since when? Wednesday?"

"Maybe, Old Man. But we're going to do this. I've already decided I'm going to put your name on the grant application. Master Sonic Manipulator."

As we went along the river, Dirk played out the scenario one more time. "I come to your concert in Osaka. Then we head up together to the New Theatre festival, where you do the soundtrack. Onstage, like before. Except this time we'll have a Hammond organ. Hammond or Wurlitzer. Or whatever. And after the first night, we'll scope for high-end prostitutes. Sorry. Forgot about Lena. *I'll* scope for prostitutes. The Ginza is where everybody says to go."

He went on. The stage setting, characters' names, the props they'd need. I was seeing it. It was becoming real to me.

As the sun began to set and the wind picked up, Dirk started calling lines from the play. "Ah! There's Lord Grandgousier arriving with his men. What are you eating now, gigantic Gargantua? Nothing, just all the veal in France. Ah! veal! veal! veal! He's eating all the veal in France!" Wind-whipped tears of laughter crossed my cheeks. For a while we walked in lockstep, our winter coats swishing against each other.

When we crossed into the newly paved roads of the townhouse complexes, Dirk stopped and turned to face me. He placed his hands on my shoulders, firmly, almost like he was holding me in place.

"Did you ever think, Old Man, why now? Why we've crossed paths at this exact moment, just as we find out we're heading to the same place?"

My teeth began to chatter.

"Cosmic fucking intervention," he said, a crack of a smile. "And Tokyo is just the beginning. There are the stages we've booked stateside. A workshop in Chicago called Hatch, where you get a grant to develop the project."

He seemed to be deliberately ignoring my own tour, as if it was secondary, but I didn't mind. I was excited.

"We *are* going to do this," he said.

"Yes."

He tightened his grip on my shoulders. "*Yes?*"

"Yes, Dirk! *Hai*, Dirk!"

He dropped his hands and tucked some stray hairs behind his ear. "Now take an address." It belonged to a friend of his in the *Gargantua* troupe, Drew, in Ithaca, New York. I was to mail everything about my trip to Drew, and he would pass it on to Dirk. When I couldn't find anything to write on, Dirk dug into his pockets, spilling a book of matches and two coins onto the ground before finding a

pen and a scrap of paper. He read out the address as he
scribbled, so I'd be able to decode when the time came. I
slipped the scrap into my wallet.

"I won't lose this," I said.

"Better not, de Vries." He pulled me towards him and
squeezed. Air escaped from his puffy jacket. A whiff of
warm skin. "The next time we'll see each other will be on
the other side of the world. Of the *planet*."

I nodded. He cupped the back of my head, like old times,
then turned around and bobbled off on his splayed feet,
moving through circles of light cast by the street lamps.
When he got to the front door of one of the farther houses,
he turned and flashed two fingers in a sign that could either
have meant "peace out" or "V for victory," which, as Dirk had
once pointed out when we were at Sint Ansfried, were two
pretty contradictory messages for a simple hand gesture.

As he opened the door I called out, "I'll see you soon!"

I arrived at Lena's parents' home as planned and immediately fit in. Far-flung branches of the family tree had
descended for the holidays and each day more neighbours
dropped by to spread the love. It was my first happy family
Christmas in ages, and I was reminded how good that felt.
An overload of food being eaten at all hours, ebbs and flows
to and from the dining room table, a present-surplussed
living room and Christmas morning gift exchange, and
even carol singing while I accompanied on the family
room upright.

But even as I joined in, being introduced and reintro-
duced to aunts and uncles and cousins and friends, riding
the fully furnished seasonal merry-go-round, I found myself
at a distance, often watching Lena. The way she spoke or
acted. The way she held or did not hold my hand. Whether
she stood right next to me or inched away in the presence
of her mother or father or little sister. I was, I realized, looking for some difference in her. Something to indicate that
there was a change in our relationship, now that I'd come
to meet her family. Or that she'd met Dirk. Something to
match my sense that we had entered a new phase. I didn't
seen any clues, but that didn't stop me looking.

For my part I put on the charm. Smiled on cue, listened
carefully, interrupted minimally, was happy to hammer
away at the keys at any invitation. But there was a part of
me that I couldn't tamp down, that was growing inside me,
slowly but steadily, like a bubble. Japan. Specific images.
A subway car gliding along a station platform. Ideogramic
lettering on a shop sign. An army of shoes marching along
crowded sidewalks. I wasn't picturing being there with
Dirk, or without Lena; I had purposely put those questions
out of my mind. Instead there were these images. At first
they were hazy, but with every recurrence they came into
sharper focus. A spare moment, a drop in the conversation,
and my mind would wander.

On the train back to Maastricht I told Lena that Dirk
was serious about meeting us. She nodded but didn't seem
particularly impressed.

"You should have seen the look on his face," I said. "He meant it."

"Are you going to send him your itinerary?"

"Yeah."

"I don't mind so long as you and I have time to ourselves," she said, elbowing me softly in the side. She turned her attention back to her book. I looked out the window to the countryside.

Back in town, with the beginning of my final term, I went back to what Lena called "the bunker," the practice rooms, where I mowed through the repertoire Taub had given me and contended with the stunning workload from the conservatory, the tutors trying to cram every last thought on performance into our heads before we were set upon the world. Once again, music took over completely. The cascading, triumphant, sometimes sarcastic chords from Debussy's *En Blanc et Noir*. The exuberant marches from Bizet's *Jeux d'Enfants*, played by two pianists on one keyboard. The percussive runs from Grieg's Norwegian Dances. Major, minor, diminished, augmented. Sostenuto, staccato, mezzo-forte, mezzo-piano, hands together, hands separate, changing keys from A to B-flat to E minor to A. Awake and asleep, I was tuned in full-time. As soon as one piece ended another began.

Then, in mid-March, a surprise. Lena and I had just begun the process of booking her tickets to Osaka when she came home from work one day to tell me she had bad news.

"All of a sudden the partners want this file done way earlier than planned. It's kind of ridiculous. Almost everyone will be putting in overtime. I'd have, at most, three days off. Barely enough time to get to Japan and back." She looked at me in disbelief. "I've been upset all day," she said. "I feel like quitting my job. Why aren't you angry?"

"How can I be angry?" I said. "This isn't your fault."

"But this is your debut I'll be missing."

"Professionally, maybe. But you saw my real premiere. At the conservatory."

She started to tear up. "I'm just so angry," she said.

Seeing her cry moved me to act. I sat us both down on the couch. "There will be other tours. Other tours to Japan, even."

"And I'll come on the next trip, right?" she said, drying her eyes. "Even if it's somewhere terrible, like, I don't know, Moldova."

"Then it'll be Moldova."

She reached for a tissue and blew her nose.

"Think about it this way," I said. "I wouldn't be on this tour if it weren't for you. All those nights in the practice room. For us."

"Do you really believe that?" she asked.

"I believe that," I said.

She nodded, indicating she believed it too. "And Dirk will be there?" she said.

"Yes."

"So you won't be alone?"

"No."

"I'm sorry I'm crying."

"Don't be sorry. You look beautiful when you cry."

"Just do me one favour," she said. "Phone from the hotel. One call before you play."

"So long as you don't hang up when the operator asks you to accept the charges."

That made her smile. We kissed. We went to the bedroom, to the bed. But afterwards, as Lena dozed next to me, I stayed fully awake. Unable to close my eyes or even to try to count sheep. Staring up at the sky, watching stars dance and wink.

One month later, though it felt like the following day, I was looking out the window of a Boeing 747, one of the new models with the stretched upper deck, en route to Osaka, Japan.

As the plane flew across the continents, over clouds and bodies of water and mountain ranges, I thought of the symphonic structure. The first movement sets out the major themes. Blustery and martial, or slow and mysterious, or lyrical and teasing. The second movement plucks one of these themes and puts it under a microscope, turning right side up to upside down, switching left and right, leaving behind the big to magnify the small. The third movement is scherzo. Just kidding! it says. It was all a joke! You couldn't possibly think any of this was serious? The fourth and final movement answers with a hammer. No! It *was* serious. It

*is* serious. It's *all* serious. The fourth recollects and ampli-
fies all the action of the previous movements. Slow-fast,
expressive-virtuosic, mysterious, calamitous, insidious,
heroic, and fateful, assembled under a building continuo
of cymbals bursting and gongs gonging. Where there are
moments of silence, they are brief and they are loud.

Which movement was I in? What was next? Was this
a new start? A new-old start? Was it a debut? A reunion?
Was I going from first to second? Second to third? Or was
it the fourth, and final, that was waiting for me?

I got in three days before the concert. Three days to get
used to the time change, including two spent rehearsing
*En Blanc et Noir* with the lead pianist, Milan Sudek, and one
spent buying a new suit. Before I left, Taub had told me the
public schoolboy look had to go. He was forwarding the
money to make it happen. That's how, on my first day in
town, I ended up at the Hankyu Department Store, picking
out a Nehru-style jacket and pants. Midnight blue. I knew it
was a ridiculous choice. But from what I could tell, Osaka
was a ridiculous place. The tall buildings along the main
street had holes in their stomachs and hats on their heads.
A tailor was summoned to mark the cuffs and hems, and I
added a collarless white shirt and black socks to the tab. I
was meant to pick up everything the day of the performance.

At the end of that first long day I unpacked my clothes
in the room and turned on the television. As the sun started
to set I walked to the window and looked out. My room
was on the tenth floor and the view was mostly rooftops

and roadways. In the distance was an elevated train track. Probably the local line, as opposed to the one that connected Osaka to other major cities. On street level the shop lights were being turned on. The sidewalks were filled with workers on their way home.

I picked up the phone, read the instructions for long-distance calling, and dialed the apartment. Nobody answered. I thought of calling again, but instead went back to the window. With a surprising suddenness, the sky had darkened; it was properly nighttime now. I would try Lena again tomorrow. Or failing that, the day of the concert. At that point my thoughts of Maastricht, the apartment, even Lena, were abstract. There was so much happening in front of me that I could barely think laterally.

I turned on the TV and sat back on the bed, trying to figure out what was happening on the screen but without much luck. What I needed, I realized, was a translator. Ridiculous-to-sensical. With many examples on hand to explain the finer points.

Rehearsal with Sudek went without a hitch. If anything, I was overprepared. The morning of the concert I woke up at eight, had breakfast in the lobby, and walked up to Hankyu. I handed in a receipt. They handed me a tan garment bag, which I slung over my shoulder. On the way back to the hotel I had what I came to realize was an "Only in Japan" moment when I saw an advertising poster of a geisha, with Marie Antoinette hair, being clobbered by a Zeppelin-sized beer. The beer was labelled, in English, "The Placenta." A man in immaculate coveralls was removing the poster from an advertising column at the entrance to a subway. Using sign language, I asked if I could have it. The man rolled it up for me and I tucked it under my arm, making a mental note to ask the hotel concierge for bubble wrap and tape.

On the day of the show there was no rehearsal, so I was free to do what I liked. I dropped off the goods in the hotel lobby and went back onto the street, spending the next couple of hours walking along the river and popping into the odd shop.

At two o'clock, I went back to my room and lifted the phone onto the bed. It felt heavy in my hands. I reread the instructions for long distance.

The phone started to ring. It was morning in Maastricht and I was expecting Lena to be a little sleepy. But when she answered she sounded like she'd been awake for a while.

The first thing she said was that I hadn't called when I got in. "I waited by the phone for hours," she said sharply.

"I made a mistake with the time difference," I said. "You were probably at the office."

"You could have tried me there."

She was right. "I don't know why I didn't think about it," I said.

Silence on her end. There was a blip on the line. The long distance.

"I'm sorry," I said, feeling stupid as the words came out but not knowing what else to say.

"I don't know," she said. "Did you really call when you said you did?"

"Yes, of course, Lena. I told you, I mixed up the time."

"And since then?"

"I've been caught up."

"You know, Jan, I've got this feeling you don't even care that I'm not there."

A stab. But the pain was localized. It didn't hurt the way I thought it would.

"Am I wrong?" she said.

"I wouldn't be here if it weren't for you."

There was a fuzzy silence. The sound of two people far away from each other.

"I've got to get ready for work," she said.

"Me too."

"Is that why you called now?" Her voice was a serrated edge. "Because we wouldn't have much time to talk?"

"I hadn't even thought about that," I said.

For a long time neither of us spoke.

"I'll be out tonight with friends," Lena said, almost absently. "The movies." The message was clear: don't call to say how it went. But before I could answer there was another blip on the line. It cut off something Lena said. The next thing I knew she'd hung up, and I was holding a dead receiver in my hand.

I put the phone aside. I'd sift through this later, I thought to myself. Her words, her anger, what she might have known, what I owed her. Even if I had wanted to reflect at the time, I couldn't. I was in a hotel room, six thousand miles away, on the cusp of my debut concert. I got up from the bed and unzipped the garment bag, which was hanging from a hook on the open bathroom door. The suit. Seemingly untouched. I brushed a hand over the jacket, the covered buttons, feeling a charge in my fingertips. I touched the jacket again, looking for another charge.

I got to the concert hall at six on the dot, one hour before curtain. The stage manager unlocked the backstage entrance for me and left me alone in the green room with a Yamaha CFIIIS, the same model as the two being lined up onstage. I lifted the fallboard and skimmed my fingers over the keys, not making a sound. In my head I could hear the score of my entire tour. Certain sections wavered. Lines switched place with other lines. A sonata borrowed a part from a concerto, then gave it back. I knew, from the experience before the showcase concert, that this was normal. When it came time to walk onstage and play the piece, muscle memory would take over.

I slid the fall back over the keys, pulled the bench from under the Yamaha, and sat down. I looked around the little room. A memory came to me. Dirk riding a pogo stick, the first I'd ever seen. Dirk didn't own it; God knows how he'd gotten it. The metal tube was blue and the rubber handles were yellow, and Dirk was pogo-ing up and down the main hall of Sint Ansfried in the middle of the day, doing impressively well right up to the point where he fell forward and smashed his head on an open locker door. He looked up at me, a red slice across his forehead, blood just starting to stream from the cut, but the expression on his face was passive, even self-impressed. "It was worth it, Old Man," he said.

Living life beyond the bounds was worth it. Squeezing excitement out of every moment no matter where it led you, no matter what calamity it brought down, was worth it. Was the whole point. Alone in the little room, I was smiling, almost laughing. I looked down at my hands, resting on the bench, and saw they were shaking with excitement.

The assistant stage manager knocked on the door to give me my five-minute warning. As if on cue, the volume of the music in my head, the opening of the Debussy, slightly increased. I stood up, checked myself in the mirror, and corrected the angle of my pocket square. Less than a minute later, I was at the stage right entrance, standing in a group with Sudek, who was wearing a dark suit and black tie, a woman holding a clipboard, and a sound technician who was gurgling into a walkie-talkie. Regular beeps sounded through the backstage, indicating the performance was about to begin.

I took a deep breath, squeezed my hands into fists, then stretched my fingers out, feeling bursts of electricity in the very tips. As I touched the buttons down the front of my jacket I felt breathing next to me. Sudek, looking out to the stage, frowning, turning away, then turning back. He broke his routine to tell me he had to go to the washroom. If he didn't come back in time, he said, I should start without him. Ha ha ha, he laughed, like a Transylvanian count, then went back to staring at the stage.

The regular beeps stopped. There was a change in the light that filtered into the wings.

He was here. I was sensing him here.

So do it, I said to myself.

At first I didn't move.

You *have* to, I repeated to myself, this time almost aloud.

Okay, fine.

I stepped away from Sudek to the edge of the wings, pulled the curtain a little farther back, and looked. Electric volts of anticipation ran clear through me. I knew where Dirk's complimentary seat was located. Around the corner from where I was standing, in a side box. "With the people who can't climb stairs," as Dirk would have put it. My breathing became shallower. My heart picked up the pace. I wanted so badly to peek around the corner, I *would* peek around the corner, but first I needed to scan some of the audience. That was my routine. I'd get to where he was sitting, I said to myself. Just start at the top.

My eyes went to the leftmost seat in the back of the hall, then zigzagged through the rows. I watched middle-aged husbands and wives, formally dressed, whispering to one another. Occasionally there was a single man or younger woman, reading a program. Very few stood out. Most of the men wore dark suits like Sudek's. All the while I kept picturing Dirk in his box. How he'd wave his arms in the air like a nutter as soon as I'd walk onstage. Histrionically bite his nails through the show. Clamour to the edge of the box when it was done, as if he was on the verge of losing his mind. Launch imaginary bouquets at the stage, as if they were hand grenades. Then Dirk and me, leaving the concert hall. The two of us heading back to the hotel together. Wired from the excitement. A new world in front of us.

*Look around the corner, Jan.*

I knew if I did that, I would be visible to the audience; I'd have to be quick.

*Look now, Jan. Before the lights go.*

I stopped scanning the rows, held my breath, and craned my neck past the curtain. I was exposed to the audience. I got a full view of the box at the very moment the house lights dimmed.

*Did you see him?*

The stage lights rose. They shone down on us even in the wings.

*Well?*

He could have been elsewhere in the audience. Maybe he didn't like his seat and took another.

*You would have seen him.*

I'd rushed through the rows. I might have missed him.

*But you didn't.*

Maybe there was some kind of emergency. Or something simpler. Missed train stop. Traffic jam. The opening bars began to speed up in my head. Runs of chords. Banging,

banging. A change of tempo. A change back. The audience was starting to applaud. I saw Sudek walk onstage in front of me and, beyond him, the white lights shining on the interlocked pianos at centre stage. My palms were sweating. A buzz ran all the way up my arms. I touched my collar, pulled at the cuffs beneath my jacket sleeves.

*He's not here.*

Onstage, the lights turned to a blinding, phosphorescent gleam. The opening bars rushed through me at an ultra-fast tempo. Prestissimo. Then ultra slow. Largo. Then both at once.

*Not here.*

I needed to divide the parts, section them off. I needed to concentrate, listen for those opening bars at the right pace, the right tone, the right volume. I needed to anticipate Sudek coming in. Change of key, change of tempo.

The applause began. I followed Sudek onstage, to the bench.

I placed my hands above the keys, and looked across the lid for Sudek's signal.

Somewhere in those few moments, the noise had evened out and quieted down. The first bars had resolved in a clear opening.

Sudek gave the signal. I struck the opening notes with force.

I landed back at Frankfurt International, on the same Boeing 747 model, three weeks later. Lena was waiting at the exit gate, as we'd arranged. She was wearing a light-coloured felt hat, with a wide brim that framed her face.

Often during the rest of the tour and constantly on the long flight home, I pictured this moment. This and others. The first time I saw Lena. Our first date. All the nights spent in the practice rooms. I'd come so close to losing her. I was angry at Dirk, of course, but wasn't it me who was responsible? I promised, over and over, I would not take her for granted again. I promised not to forget what I had almost lost.

When Lena saw me through the doors, she broke into a beautiful, heart-melting smile. After more than twelve hours of travel, whatever doubts and fears I had built in anticipation instantly faded. I felt that I was hers again. That nothing had changed.

"I picked up a hot chocolate for you," she said. "There's a Lindt and Sprüngli stand in the terminal, if you can believe it. It's still steaming, so be careful." We went to the baggage carousel, where I grabbed my checked bag, then to the curb, where we joined the line for limos into the city. Her eyes were alert, her hand gripping mine.

We glided into Frankfurt along dusky streets. Lena had booked us a hotel room downtown, near the Museumsufer. She had also booked us dinner, she said, but on second thought nixed it. "We're going to have room service," she said in a decidedly self-possessed way. "I've vetted the menu."

She paid the limo driver with a credit card, which had apparently come in the mail while I was away. I asked her if she'd used it to pay for the new hat. "This," she said, taking the hat off and admiring it, "came from a store on the Wolfstraat."

"I think I know which one," I said.

We squeezed into a small elevator with our luggage and the porter. For a second, in the uncomfortable proximity, something was off. I caught it in Lena's face. An uncertainty. But once we were in the room, Lena went about busying with drawers and curtains and running the bath and things went back to normal.

By the time I got out of my bath, the meal had arrived. Lena had taken the dishes off the trays and spread them over the bed. Not like her to encourage mess-making, but we were on holiday. The second I sat on the bed, though, I started to lose steam. "Do you mind if I just take a break for a sec and close my eyes?" I asked. Lena leaned forward and kissed me on the lips. "Do what you want," she said. Those were her last words before I drifted into jet-lagged dreamland.

I awoke later that night, and sat up in bed. The clock showed five in the morning. The room was dark, but I could see well enough to notice the plates of food had been cleared off the bed. As I turned next to me, I heard Lena move. She was awake too.

"I'm sorry," I whispered.

"No, *I'm* sorry," she said.

I shook my head. I didn't understand.

"For what I said on the phone," she said. "I regretted it the moment I said it. These last three weeks, being out of touch . . ."

"Me too," I said.

"I didn't think it would be this hard," she said, sniffling. She slipped her fingers between mine. I squeezed.

"I'm sorry too," I said. "I realized, while I was away, I'd taken you for granted."

Lena seemed to ignore my words. "You need the space to practise and work. I know that, I just had this feeling, while you were away, there was something wrong. Actually it had been building for months, and I only realized it after the call."

I shook my head.

"There's nothing," I said.

"I didn't ruin the debut for you?"

"No, my love. You couldn't ruin anything for me."

I lay down next to her. Our faces inches from each other. She was breathing from her mouth into my nose. It smelled sweetly of her morning breath. I could never get enough of it. She didn't believe me when I had told her this, and she subsequently rolled away from me whenever she noticed I was timing my inhales with her exhales, but it was true.

"Will you tell me everything, Jan?" she said, breathing sweetly. "From the beginning of the tour? The hotel room? The concert hall in Osaka? Everything?"

We kissed.

"What do you want to know?" I asked.

"Come on, Jan," she said, "you know I love details. First international performance. Four-city tour. Different country. Different *continent*. Tell me *something*."

I scanned over the trip, starting to feel drowsy again. I told her about the strangely high-pitched voices of the women I spoke to, about the soup in a pouch called *ramen*, about how televisions in hotel rooms were easy to turn on but impossible to shut off.

"And Dirk?" she asked. "How did it turn out with him? His festival?"

"He came to Osaka for the performance, then went back to Tokyo for his show."

"You didn't go with?"

"No," I said. "Couldn't fit it in the schedule."

"It always seemed like a long shot," Lena said. "But at least you weren't alone for the debut."

"No," I said. "I wasn't."

She asked for more on the performances themselves. What the soloists were like. The orchestra members.

She moved closer. I slid my hand down to her waist, her hips.

"I don't want to fight again," she said.

"We won't," I answered. "Ever. At least, not about this."

We kissed again.

A few hours later we got out of bed. I drew the curtains and packed our bags as Lena took a shower. On the train ride to Maastricht, Lena turned to me and in the same confident voice she'd had the night before, said that while I was away she'd often remembered how she used to come home from the office and find me staring out the window. Was she thinking I should move in? I asked. Not thinking, she said. Telling.

As far as I was concerned, that was the story. Dirk came and shortly after he left. A lie that, to me, weighed the same as truth. If, after my first night back, Lena thought about our fight, I didn't catch a whiff of it. She had moved on. I did too.

As time passed, I heard from Dirk again. Once a year, for the better part of the following ten years, I'd get a postcard from him. The first were forwarded from my dorm, but eventually they came direct. Usually around my birthday, Christmas, or New Year's. I found the first when I got back from a tour, with Lena, of Moscow and Leningrad. It had a picture with the caption "Sunrise in Lapland"; it looked like a generic mailer, something from a cruise operator. On the back was written "Happy Birthday, Jan. I hope you have an excellent year." I tore the card in half, but regretted it right away. I taped the halves together and slipped it into the old shoebox, where I kept all the Sint Ansfried things.

The next Christmas I received another postcard. An oil painting of palm trees overlaid by the words "Happy New Year" in loopy script. It arrived shortly after I came back from a recording session in Germany. On the reverse side was the familiar chicken scratch. "Have a good one. Sincerely, D."

In the shoebox.

The next year was a note extending "Good tidings for the season." Then came a letter on my grandmother's passing; I didn't know how he heard. He sent congratulations when I was profiled in a long article in one of the Sunday magazines, and another when my first credit on a major label, Sony, came out. They were always one-liners. Never any personal information. No requests to write back. Not even a return address. None made much of an impression. All went straight into the shoebox.

At the beginning of my career, I made so little money it was laughable. The first tour, to Japan and Korea, was by far the most lucrative. After that the dates were spread thin and I had to teach at the conservatory, when there was an opening, and give private lessons, mostly to children. Not once during that time, even during our fights, which were rare and usually about housekeeping, did Lena bring up the disparity in our income or complain about my lack of financial success. She took pride in every date I booked, big and small. When her friends from work got engaged to men with professions and regular paycheques, Lena never hinted that she regarded my artistic pursuit as less digni-fied than any other kind of career, and dismissed the idea any time I brought it up, which was usually out of guilt. When I asked her about children, whether she was holding back because I wasn't bringing enough in, she reminded me that when we started dating she said she didn't want children. Had she changed her mind, though?

"It won't always be this way," I said. "I might start picking up dates, travelling more often. Won't you want someone in the house while I'm gone?"

She hadn't changed her mind, she said.

Among musician friends and acquaintances, I heard stories of long-suffering partners who left after it dawned on them that their other halves were never going to catch that break, and that their life together was not going to turn out as expected. I just listened. That, I knew, was not going to happen me.

In the meantime, Lena worked long hours. She worked on the weekend when the boss asked, and her effort and intelligence gradually gained notice. When she got her first promotion, the year she turned thirty, we left the apartment for the upper two storeys of a house in a more established part of Maastricht. It gave a similar view of the river and the old city with the walls curling around it, but on clear days you could also look south across the border to Belgium and the hills that sprouted from the loosening topography. The new place had three bedrooms, and shortly after moving in, while I was on one of my longer tours, Lena had the third room soundproofed and installed a forty-eight-inch K-400 upright Kawai. I came home to a practice room of my own, which was in itself a great surprise, but what I remember best was Lena's reaction. As I felt the soundproofing and examined the upright, she stood by the door bouncing on her tiptoes, a kid who found the present she'd wished for under the tree.

It was for the loyalty, generosity, and excitement that Lena gave me, and for all I owed her in return, that I kept to myself the whirr of sounds that were increasingly part of life. The music that came and went while I practised, the unusual sounds I heard while on a walk or during a lesson. Not that they seriously concerned me. I'd heard music playing in my head since I was a student at the conservatory, and I'd accepted and even welcomed these strange sounds as a secondary voice. If they were now amplified pre-concert, which they were, I figured it was a form of stage fright, which was, as far as I could tell, part of being a musician. I had heard stories of hyperventilation, light-headedness, cold hands, tremors, even blackouts. Sometimes temporary, sometimes permanent; all worse, to my mind, than what was happening to me. The experience backstage in Osaka was an extreme case, there were other factors to account for, and even then what I heard hadn't gotten in the way of my performing.

❖

The gift of the Kawai marked the beginning of a new stage in my career. Shortly after I started practising on it, I said to Lena, "Do you remember that time, before the run-up to the showcase concert, when I kept regular hours?"

"Before you decided to disappear into the bunker?"

"I'm going back to keeping those hours," I said. "I've been living off bad student habits too long. I haven't developed. I'm serious about this. Will you help me?"

"Anything I can do," she said, more excited than I was.

From then on, while most of my peers went on living the chaotic lives of sessional musicians, staying up all night and sleeping through most of the day, Lena made sure I went to bed and got up at a good time. We talked over breakfast about my goals, short- and long-term. When she left for the office, my clock started. There might be a phone call over lunch, but otherwise I was alone for the day.

A typical practice day began with technical work. Warming the fingers with scales and chords and Hanons. Circulating the blood and loosening the joints. After the fingers, I'd warm up the piano. Run trills and glissandi up and down the keyboard. Crack the lower register as if prodding a beast. Listen for the hum that rises off the cast-iron soundboard, the sign that the instrument's vocal cords are vibrating on their own.

I'd review notes from the previous day. Transition to new key. Soft staccato in left. Dynamics in the last three bars. I'd add ideas that might have come to me at night or from chatting with Lena. Una corda pedal in the second section. Hold the A minor longer in the left. Last word to the lower chord. But I didn't dwell on them. When I was a student at the conservatory I could spend hours in front of a keyboard playing out fantasies or days in front of a record player sampling interpretations by past masters. If I wanted to, I could spend three weeks on a passage of Ravel, or engage in a term-long discussion with a tutor about Saint-Saëns' idiosyncratic phrasing. We could argue about whether the score was sacred or improvisation was allowed. Whether one plays in period or updates for the modern age. But if I was going to be a professional I would have to keep a professional's schedule. No more poet waiting for his inspiration. Learn the section, choose an interpretation, stick with it, move to the next section. If I had imposed this routine on my student self, I would have rebelled. But as it became the outline of my daily life, and I added more pieces to my repertoire, and took on more work as a result, I found I liked it.

Lena liked it too. When she'd get home, I'd leave the keyboard behind. I'd have nights free to go to the cinema or on double dates at restaurants with her friends. I'd be available to pick her up from the office if she worked late, or sit and read in the chair across from her desk till she finished a file. She liked it when I showed up there, her man who looked rested and contented, was well travelled and sometimes named in the newspaper or culture magazines. Not a lawyer, like the other office spouses; her musician.

❖

To Taub I give credit for the second ingredient of my success.

Back when I was a child starting to learn, I thought of myself as a musician. Then, a pianist. In high school, I daydreamed of recording *Pictures at an Exhibition*, forming a quintet, and retiring every summer to a cabin in the woods, maybe the Finnish woods, à la Jean Sibelius. Over the years in the conservatory, I became drawn to certain periods and styles, and by the end narrowed my focus to Romantic music, mostly French. And in the early years of my professional career, Taub refashioned me again, this time as an accompanist, specializing in the French Romantic. "Be a big fish in a small pond," he said at one of the meetings in his office. "It'll pay off, you'll see." I seethed all day till Lena got home. When I told her Taub's plan, I was sure she would side with me, but she didn't.

"How can you not see he's right?" Lena asked.

"But don't you think this is a step back?" I said.

"From what? Waiting for Taub to call, an opening at the conservatory? Won't you be onstage more, working more?"

"Yes, but as an accompanist?"

"So what you're saying is you'll be part of a jam session every time you show up to work?"

"Not exactly. I'll be the person in the shadows."

"Not to me, you won't. You'll be the person who played with this famous violist or cellist or other pianist. Who accompanied them. Who was part of their performance as much as they were part of yours."

"Coming out of the conservatory," I said, "all I could see was potential. Big stages, bright lights. This is not what I pictured."

"The reality," Lena said, "is that you're young. You've been playing professionally, what, five years? You could be playing another forty or fifty. If Taub thinks this is how you'll make your name, you should trust him. This is what he knows."

I had no answer.

"Come on, Jan," she said. "You know I'm right."

I started to thaw.

"You *know* I'm right," she said.

Lena was right. Taub was right. I wasn't Midori or Evgeny Kissin, prodigies who debuted in their preteens. It was not only that I needed to work harder than others, which I already knew; I needed to find my own route to success.

The surprise was in how naturally the role came to me. Accompaniment is a particular skill. You are the bridge between the audience and the soloist, a lens that magnifies the leading melody, a handler to the outsized personality next to you, one player who sometimes has to be two. While soloist and accompanist are meant to have worked through variations on the piece before a performance, reality is more often a limited number of rehearsals crammed into a half-week before the show. There were even times when I would have to play on the fly, using my knowledge of a soloist's previous performances and musical proclivities. How strict or flamboyant is the soloist, how technically adept or concerned with atmosphere? Is he or she given to moments of improvisation or devoted to the music as sacred script? Light on the fingers or tending to heavy weather? Showman or cold fish?

This was where the other soundtrack that played in my head came into it. While I practised on my own parts of the piece, I could hear, during breaks and occasionally even while I played, a second voice. It could be the soloist's part, an alternative take on the entire piece, or a piece I'd played long ago that my mind was telling me had something to do with what I was working on now. I'd been cast as accompanist for as long as I could recall, only I hadn't known it. The sounds in my head were tutor, bandmate, producer, a studio at work, mixing tracks and adjusting levels. Whether Taub was merely being opportunistic, like any good agent, or saw something in my playing that made me good for the part, I couldn't say. But he'd been right.

I was in my mid-thirties when Taub started booking me into A-list venues. "You've climbed a rung," he said to me at another meeting in his offices. "It's hard to know when, these things are a bit of alchemy. But some good advice probably came into it." He bit at the end of his cigarillo and cocked one of his eyebrows.

As my calendar started filling up, I was being booked months, and soon years, in advance. I was becoming some-one. Putting on weight. Getting a little *fat*. A performance with the Concertgebouw or review in the national paper went from being events worthy of celebration to matters of routine. I had dates to play the second piano with Buchbinder, to accompany Shaham and Honoré, and perform at Wigmore Hall with Fischer-Dieskau. My name graced the marquee at the Salle Pleyel, in Paris, and the Musikverein, in Vienna. I even headlined a series of my own performances and released my own album. What would have been unbelievable to me, just a few years prior, was becoming normal.

At the end of a particularly successful tour with several sold-out audiences in major halls, the year I turned thirty-six, I wanted to do something special with Lena. I felt I was on a mountain peak. Taub kept telling me trajectory was everything in the business, and that I needed to keep climbing. But was there really another flight up?

I had Taub arrange for a week off after the last show, which was in Paris, and for Lena to come and meet me. Ten years before, Lena and I had gone to a small restaurant on the Quai de Conti. Back then, it was a taste of the life that might be. Too extravagant, too expensive, but worth it. Now I made reservations to go back.

In anticipation, Lena had her hair cut at a Paris salon recommended by the company manager, and was wearing a new black dress. Her lips were bright red and her nails polished to match. When she met me in the green room after the curtains, she turned heads, but we barely spoke to others because we were eager to slip away.

It was close to ten when the taxi dropped us on the sidewalk in front of the restaurant. I held the car door open while Lena dispensed the francs. We crossed the small street arm in arm. Though my ears were still buzzing from two hours onstage, I could hear her heels clicking along the pavement.

We were fit in with the last seating. The restaurant's small dining room, packed with tables, was full. Lena ordered drinks. For a long time neither of us spoke, we just took in the scene. Table, room, city, the night that had just passed. How far we'd come.

Last time at the restaurant we'd been cheap. This time we ordered everything. The courses streamed in. Amuses-gueules, soups, salads, meats, sweets. "Exactly as good as last time," Lena said. "Except with more foam."

I lost track of time. The tables around us started clearing out. As Lena was watching me polish off the last dessert from a sample plate, an older couple next to us got up to leave. As they passed by, the man put his hand on our table and leaned towards me while looking at Lena.

"You have a beautiful wife," he said in English.

I looked at the woman who was with him. She smiled and nodded.

The couple left. I suddenly reached for Lena's hands and pulled them towards me.

"I love you, Lena."

"I love you, too, Jan de Vries," she said.

I thought to myself, Where would I be without her? Lena looked at me with what seemed like unlimited tenderness. I intertwined my fingers in hers.

Bubbles appeared at the table; I don't know who ordered them. After that, we were each given a glass of dessert wine on the house. Soon the room emptied out. The staff started cleaning up, switching off lights, overturning chairs. I was wiped. It was a long tour. My ears, ringing earlier, were now barking. Too much to eat. Too much to drink. But there was one thing I wanted to do.

I wanted, in that moment, to preserve what I saw. So I drew myself up in my chair, focused my mind, set a square around Lena, like a frame, and studied everything inside that frame. The background. Dim dining room, chairs on top of tables, low-hanging ceiling lamps. The foreground. Our table, its marked-up tablecloth and napkins, the wineglasses and flutes, Lena's leather clutch set on the edge. Then Lena. Her skin as smooth and pale as the day I saw her at the bar. Long fingers, with polished nails, half covering her mouth. The unblemished whites of her eyes around the dark irises. Her perfect teeth. The slight rise of her chest with each inhale.

"What are you *doing*?"

"Shh," I said. "Nothing."

I didn't want her to move, or change. I wanted that exact moment. To keep it with me, take it wherever I went. A kind of talisman. A protection. A light.

Three years later, Lena and I were standing on the small street in front of the house on a cool but sunny morning, watching workmen use a crane to move the body of a baby grand walnut Bechstein, Model A, up the face of the building. A loan from a benefactor. Out of the blue I got a call at the apartment, was asked if I had the space to accommodate a baby grand, and when I said yes, I was told to come to a law office to sign papers, which Lena reviewed. We had the Kawai removed the next day.

After the body of the Bechstein was guided through the third-floor window, workmen came up the stairs with the lid, drop, music shelf, pedal box, legs, and casters. They were followed by the tuner, who worked for the rest of the morning, as I watched and asked questions, thinking one day I might learn to tune myself, although pianists are known among musicians for having the least knowledge of the instruments they play.

Lena was giddy as she watched the buzzing around the baby grand, and after the workers left she and I closely examined the instrument itself. The light colour, walnut inlay, carved legs. Going from a Kawai upright to a Bechstein was like moving up a major fifth, the sound that blasts from the trumpets when the king is crowned, when the winner is announced; the flush of triumph.

But that feeling only lasted a short time. It must have been coincidence, there's no possibility the Bechstein itself made me sick, but soon after it took over the practice room, the auditory disruptions I was hearing became more acute. They'd start in the morning, before I was even seated at the keyboard. Contractions and minor spasms that seeped down the back of my head, to my neck, shoulders, and arms. There were times, while practising, when confused and clashing notes seemed to buzz across my eyes and catch in my throat. Taking a break to work on scales or other technical warm-ups, I'd hear a piece I'd played a week or month or even years before return at full volume, opening the door to a slew of other vagabond sounds. My response was to play through it, to overrun it with work. I practised more hours and booked more dates. I cleaved ever more closely to my routine. The more I had to do, the less possible it was for me to pause, never mind stop, and this was meant to keep the threatening sounds under my control.

There was another thing that troubled my success at the time, also bothersome, also out of my control. The more I toured, the more I seemed to run into old friends and acquaintances from the Sint Ansfried years. Members of the diaspora who were in orchestras or crews or management, or simply in the audience on a given night. Now that I was a name, they wanted a piece, and took every chance to press themselves on me. Which in its own way brought

Dirk back because after hellos and how are yous, I'd always get asked the same question. "How is the old Noosen?"

I had a tactic for this: smile at the question, then wait till the person asking told what he or she had heard. And that person, whoever he or she was, had always heard something. "He was in New York City," they'd say. Or "Buenos Aires." "The Edinburgh Festival," said another. "What? No! The London Academy." One year he was teaching at the Sorbonne. The next it was apprenticing with Greenaway in the West End. Assisting Stoppard, on Broadway, they said. No, off-Broadway. No, off-off-Broadway. He's riding the back lanes of some godforsaken country in an overstuffed jeep. Some pilot project that involved hacking away at jungle vines just to scrounge out a stage for his latest production. He was acting, directing, and producing. One person was aware, first-hand, that he was artist-in-residence at one of those Hudson River colleges. "Or was it the Southwest?" "Certainly in America," someone else said. "Certainly not." They'd heard he was doing three productions of *Gargantua Redux* on three continents, simultaneously. Workshopping a musical parody of *Hair* called *Hairy*. Then there was that television interview that caused such a scandal. "He was talking about New Theatre and late-stage communism—did you catch it?" "Yeah, that one," I'd say. "Amazing, eh?" "Typical."

I treated these bits of unbidden news like grace notes, no less or more important than the other noises whizzing through my head at the time. A dusty prelude, the snap of a Sam and Dave drumbeat, high notes from a Vaughan Williams suite, and now Dirk in some far-off jungle. I filed the information away, but didn't go further down the trail. Didn't want to. Sometimes a detail, the name of a production he was working on, or city he'd last been seen in, replayed itself in my mind during those short but wild moments while I scanned the rows before a performance, but when the stage lights rose I turned my focus exclusively to the first bar, which always came to me, if only at the last minute.

My life on tour consisted of stretches like Hanover on a Tuesday, Paris on Thursday, Lisbon on Friday. Then San Francisco, Minnesota, Rio de Janeiro, and Tel Aviv in the next ten days. Whenever I checked in with Lena, I always had some bit of news to offer, but onstage it was the same pieces, same instruments, and offstage, the same routine. Hours at the bench, keeping up my schedule no matter where I was, turning down the invitation to go out with other musicians because tomorrow was an early day.

As busy as I was, as little time as work gave me to think and reflect, I began to see, as I turned forty, that the bubbling, roiling sounds that were with me day and night were not the same noises that followed me in the conservatory and during the early days of touring. These new disruptions were not yet curbing my ability to practise, and they didn't follow me onstage or disrupt my performance, but they were growing more demanding at other times. Midday, when I got up from the bench to make myself a snack in the kitchen. Afternoons, when I left the apartment to walk along the Maas. In the evenings I could hear them while Lena and I were eating at the dinner table. In bed, while she was asleep, I lay listening to what sounded like a radio with poor reception, or a fight in the apartment next door, even though there was no radio on and no apartment next door.

With every passing month, I began to worry a little more. I started to consider the possibility that these were symptoms of a condition that needed attention. I considered telling Lena, but remembered the reasons I had long ago decided against it. If I brought it up now she'd ask why I'd kept it for so long to myself. I didn't want to explain, and I was sure I could take care of whatever was the matter myself.

I started to "take care of the matter" by experimenting with simple, obvious changes. I cut down on alcohol, took sleeping pills, and bought noise-cancelling headphones for flights. While away from the keyboard, I put cotton balls in my ears and turned the kitchen radio to a murmuring low. I took showers rather than baths because of the soothing clatter of falling water. And when I stayed in hotel rooms while on tour, I played white noise tapes on a portable stereo. *Calming Javanese Waterfalls*, *Trickling Rivers of the High Andes*, and my preferred, *Dishwasher Cycles*. I kept a diary, making notes of when the symptoms got better or worse. Was it a certain season? A type of weather?

Finally, when I needed perspective, I reminded myself I played from a set repertoire I had performed dozens, and sometimes hundreds, of times, which I could play backwards and forwards, skipping every even or odd note if need be. I reasoned that so long as I was intact onstage, I could go on keeping my condition to myself. And from my old discussions with other musicians who put up with all kinds of exotic symptoms and ailments from broad travel and stressful schedules, it seemed entirely possible I would wake up one day and find everything in its proper place. A day when I'd get out of bed to a quiet breakfast with Lena, and calmly read the morning papers. When I'd sit at the Bechstein and find an immediate balance between the force from my fingers and the response from the keys. When what I'd hear in my head would combine effortlessly with the notes coming from the piano.

I waited for that day to come. I waited longer. Months passed. Soon it was years.

One by one, the cotton balls, white noise tapes, and other homemade cures stopped working. The diary told me nothing. My noise-cancelling earphones no longer made a dent. My answer was to get Taub to concentrate my dates and cut down the amount of travel because each time I boarded a plane I felt the pressure change was doing me harm.

When Lena noticed the cancellations and alterations to my schedule, she asked what was up. I told her I was taking a short rest. At first she didn't understand. Then she thought I was kidding. Rests, pauses, even during a concerto movement, were not part of her Jan. She asked if I was going to take up a hobby instead. Watercolours or knitting. When she saw her jokes irritated me, her smile fell, which is what I had wanted to avoid. I tried to calm her down.

"The travelling," I said. "It's been heavy this past year."

"That's all it is?" Lena said.

"Yes. And maybe the business side, too."

"What are you telling me?"

"I'm starting to feel wiped out."

Her voice rose. "Are you saying you want to *quit*?"

I had tripped myself up. Said too much. "That's not what I mean," I said. I looked away, but could feel Lena's eyes on me. "Just, a break would be nice."

"All right, Jan. Just so long as that's all it is."

"I'll be fine."

She was still frowning at me. Uncertainty.

"I promise," I said, thinking of what I might say to change the subject.

With more time between tours, I tried to slip into my old life. The one before I was booked solid, with a pre-played future. The days when Lena and I would sleep in on weekends, visit the patisserie together on Sunday morning and spend the rest of the day trying, and failing, to cook something in the kitchen. I see I was looking for her, in some way, to be the solution to the problem. And for the first months I expected she would be, that her love for me and my love for her would take me back.

At Christmas, during the lucrative *Ode to Joy* season, I made an appointment at the audiology department of the Academic Hospital. The testing centre did not require referrals, so I could keep the visit to myself.

The clinic's waiting room was as anonymous looking as the lobby of an insurance office. If it hadn't said Head and Neck Surgery on the door across the hall I wouldn't have known I was in a hospital. I checked myself in and recited the basics to the receptionist. Jan de Vries, forty-three, musician, no allergies, here for range testing. I signed at the bottom of the completed form.

A nurse led me to a room with a small desk, on which there was a tape recorder. Sit there, sir. Put these head-phones on. Lift your left or right arm to show me which side the sound's coming from.

I went to a room with a foam-lined booth, the same foam as in the practice room at my apartment. "You will hear beeps," said a voice coming through speakers hidden behind the foam. "Lift an arm when you stop hearing them."

In an examination room, a technician used an oto-scope to look into my ears while asking if I had had any infections as a child. None that I know of, I said. He changed the setting on his instrument and checked again.

"The good news," he said, though without much joy, "is that nothing is jumping out. According to the printout from the tests, you're within normal range." He put his tools away, filed some papers in a folder, and gave me a plastic syringe. "In case it recurs," he said, "fill the tube with a solution of sodium bicarbonate and glycerine, which you can get at any pharmacy, and slowly empty it into your ear canals."

Despite the technician's unpromising tone, I felt better instantly. I'd scientifically tested my fears and the results were fine. Good. Normal. The buoyancy lasted a month. Blissfully peaceful, one *Ode to Joy* after another without any symptoms. Then the trouble returned, worse than before. It came in the form of all kinds of noises now. A kettle on the boil. A child's piercing scream. An impatient driver blasting his horn. It was as though they were all turning against me.

I went back to the clinic and was referred to the doctor in charge. This man, an ear, nose, and throat specialist, reviewed my case, did some cursory examinations, then asked if I was familiar with the term "auditory attacks." I said I wasn't, and that it sounded bad.

"'Good' and 'bad,'" he said, "don't come into it."

He scheduled more tests. Different tests, he said. They'd have to be done in a series. On the way out the door I took some pamphlets. Each was slightly different, but all were about how a normal brain screens everyday noises behind internally generated sounds, and how sometimes the screening mechanism overreacts. They emphasized, repeatedly, that nobody's sure why this was so, and that brain activity is not fully understood.

For the first time I was scared. I started to hear a persistent whine, like a child scratching at a violin. The harmonies I wanted to latch on to while practising would break into clashing parts, and the random disruptions started to eat into my confidence at the keyboard. What exactly was I playing if I couldn't be entirely sure what I was hearing?

One afternoon, I sat at the computer. A mostly neglected piece of equipment in the house. As useless as the pamphlets from the audiologist were, they got me wanting more information. As the son of a doctor I knew not to trust what I found on the internet, but I decided to take a quick look anyway. My idea was to visit a couple of reliable-seeming sites, but I was instantly drawn in. A single search on "auditory attacks" led to pages on oversensitive membranes, infections, tinnitus, cancer of the acoustic nerve, lesions, vertigo, brain damage, damage to the cochlea, the labyrinth, the eardrum. Apparently any of these could be the cause of my problems, and further complications could include seizures or strokes. I found virtual communities where people described symptoms, suggested remedies, and charted their decline. I recognized myself in many of the symptoms listed and grew afraid of others. Inability to sleep, problems with eyesight, frequent loss of balance. Partial or complete deafness. After logging off I could barely rouse myself. What was the point? I only snapped back to life when, minutes before Lena was due to come home, a corner of my brain remembered to erase my tracks on the computer.

Over the coming months I went back to the clinic for more advanced tests. I was passed to a neurologist at the Academic. In the following year of consultations, spread between my concert dates, the number of doctors multiplied. ENTs, radiologists, surgeons, and internists. A neurosurgeon who consulted with the neurologists; a radiologist brought on as an advisor; a psychiatrist who wanted me to try medications. Each had his or her own diagnosis and solution. I went back for more in-depth testing. The results came back, calling for more tests, which I attended, always alone.

Secrecy, firewalls, containment, bright white lines notwithstanding, it was only a matter of time till Lena picked up on something, and it happened when she heard a message left by a doctor's secretary on our answering machine. I heard Lena play it and my heart sagged. When we were in bed that night she asked about it. An appointment at the hospital? I told her I'd been having headaches that weren't going away. There was a GP who was going to take a look. Right away I regretted saying it.

"I thought your slower schedule was doing you good," she said.

"It is. I'm getting better. I don't think this thing's connected."

"Describe it," she said.

I waved at her. "Like I said, headaches," I said. "And sometimes a ringing afterwards."

"Is it bothering your playing?" she said, sounding more alarmed.

"Nothing like that, no. I just wish it weren't there so often."

"*How* often?"

"I don't know."

"Now and then, or all the time?"

"Not all the time, no. Sometimes it just feels like that."

She was quiet. I resisted the urge to elaborate or to soothe her with words; too many had already come out wrong. All the while I feared her asking the question: how long has this been going on? But in trying to avoid it, I'd led myself into another corner. Lena turned to me and said that someone at the firm, one of the partners, had seen a specialist. "The partner did a lot of research to find this doctor. Apparently he's at the top of the field. I don't want you to worry about this, Jan, but he's a neurologist."

"A neurologist," I repeated. "I don't think I'm there yet but, out of curiosity, did he help the partner?"

"Yes," Lena said. "A number of specialists told him there was nothing to be done about his headaches, but this doctor found something. I can't remember the name of it. A neuroma, maybe? The doctor saw it before others did, had it operated on, and now he's better."

"That's good," I said.

"The doctor's name was Weetman. If I get his number, I want you to make the appointment, okay? Even if you don't need it now. There's a long wait list, so just sign up. People come to him from around the world. So call as soon as you can, yes?"

"Yes," I said, trying to seem offhanded about it.

When I mentioned Weetman's name to my other doctors, they said he was excellent and they would have referred me to him in time. Outstanding, world-class; risk taking but frequently right. The waiting list for an introductory consultation was actually eighteen months, but I had strings pulled on my behalf and would see him within the year.

In the meantime, I kept to my reduced performance schedule. Made fewer plane trips. Did a lot of "drive-by" concerts, with minimal rehearsal before going onstage. Lena saw I was working, which seemed to reassure her. When she asked how I was feeling, I told her it was better. I had made the appointment with Weetman, I said, though I'm sure I'd be fine by the time I showed up at his office. "Like when you call a repairman and the problem solves itself while he's on the way over."

I started seeing Weetman at his offices on the Sporenstraat later that year, shortly after I turned forty-four. The first thing to do, he said, is to start over. Establish a new baseline. All previous tests would be retaken, samples resubmitted, old analyses run alongside new. If you think this is a waste of time, he said to me, a real waste of time would be proceeding on the basis of previous results. Over the following months I would be hooked up to sensors, placed in chambers, prodded, measured, expanded, contracted, high, low, top, bottom, left, right, come and go. Move this way; now that. Hold still. Keep holding.

I went back, again, to picturing the perfect day I had laid out for myself. The one where I woke up to a noiseless solitude, and the only music playing inside my head was what came from the piano. Weetman was young and brash, but not unkind. In the minds of his peers, he was the best of the best. For me, he was the last stop.

Still, I can't say what course I might have taken had I not run into Pirm. Skinny Pirm from Sint Ansfried, who had since grown a pot-belly and wore his hair slicked back. He'd climbed the rungs at the Ministry of Education, Culture and Science, where he sat on committees and boards, travelled as an attaché, and appeared in cultural programs on TV. I had run across him several times over the years, and each time he was bigger and swarthier. Talk between us was usually limited to school days, parties, and his adventures using and dealing drugs. This time, I ran into him at a restaurant in the old city, where I'd been having dinner with Lena. Lena was paying the bill and I was collecting our coats from a stand by the door.

"Jan! Little de Vries!"

I looked around and spotted the familiar face at the bar. I could tell from the redness of his nose and untucked shirt that he'd had plenty to drink.

"Join me for a nightcap, old boy."

I shook my head.

"Oh, *come on*, de Vries," he said.

He extended his arm towards me. I looked back at Lena, who was still at the table, waiting for the receipt.

"Okay," I said. "A shot of gin."

"A *single* shot? Just the one? Okay."

Pirm was one of the few who did not ask immediately about Dirk. Maybe he had some inclination. Maybe he preferred to talk about himself. I listened as he rambled about a junket to Shanghai and his opinions on the worldwide transfer of wealth or something like that. The room was loud and hearing him was difficult. But I kept nodding while checking on Lena. She'd recognized a couple she knew and was standing next to their table. The bartender came back with two gins on the rocks. I took a small sip from my glass and replaced it on the bar. I was about to thank Pirm, who made a show of paying, and to make my apologies for leaving, when he said, "Funny thing. Dirk applied for funding from the ministry. Something about bringing Eastern practices like Noh theatre into his program. I think it was Noh theatre. Fucked if I remember."

I did not understand what Pirm was talking about, though I wasn't really trying.

"He was on about Claude Debussy's fascination with

Indonesian gamelan and its 'profound influence' on *Clair de Lune*."

"Reminds me of something I wrote for my Maastricht application," I said.

"Ha," Pirm said. "Classic Dirk."

He signalled to the bartender for a top-up, then leaned in. His breath stunk.

"Out of curiosity," he said, "when was the last time you actually, you know, spoke to him?"

I tilted my head but didn't answer. He repeated the question. I looked away and shrugged.

"Come on, de Vries, just tell me the last time you spoke to him."

"A while ago," I said.

"A while? Like a few months?"

I shook my head again.

Pirm nodded. Maybe he understood, maybe he didn't. I was tired and didn't care either way. Lena had sat down at the table with the couple. She didn't look like she was staying too long, but neither did she look eager to leave.

Pirm took a long sip from a new drink, then pulled a handkerchief from his breast pocket and wiped a line of sweat from his forehead.

"It's funny how these things go, de Vries."

I cleared my throat. "What things?" I said.

"You and Dirk. I might've guessed you two would fall out of touch completely, but it could've been the opposite. Care to fill me in?"

"It's nothing, really," I said.

Pirm smiled and shook his head slowly. "You know, Jan, we all thought you two were . . ." He grinned.

I waited for him to finish his sentence, but he was waiting for me to prod him. After a pause, I gave in.

"Us two?" I said.

"Yes, you two," he said. "You know, *you two* . . ."

"Us two *what*?" I said.

"Well, everyone in Sint Ansfried figured you and Dirk were . . . *you know*."

He elbowed me in the ribs, to underline the point. It dawned on me what Pirm meant. I felt my face flush.

"The sleepovers," he said. "Always attached at the hip, as it were . . . It was quite obvious, really."

I looked over to Lena. She was still talking but sitting on the edge of her seat. Maybe getting ready to leave. Pirm went on. "It was obvious that Dirk was in love with you. That's what everyone thought, anyway."

My mouth opened. Nothing came. I ran over Pirm's words, to make sure I had heard them right, and felt my face grow redder. Pirm wiped a fresh bead of sweat from his brow.

"Well, that's why Dirk left, isn't it? *America*. He made out like it was a lifelong ambition, but I'd known him since grade seven and he never said anything about it. *I* think it was his parents' idea. Fresh start."

"I wouldn't know about that," I said.

"How else do you explain his breakdown that first year?"

"Breakdown?"

Pirm cleared his throat, leaned in even closer. "You didn't know any of this? Nobody told you?" Pirm took a sip from his glass. "Apparently, he spent nights wandering around the city. One time his roommate found him sitting on the edge of a suspension bridge."

I couldn't fathom what Pirm was saying. Dirk on a bridge? Dirk *alone*? I felt the prick of a dagger in my heart. Out of the corner of my eye I saw Lena stand up and say goodbye to her friends.

"And I suppose you didn't know he dropped out halfway through his senior year? He only got his degree years later in Delft."

Pirm's words were like little flashes in the dark, too quick to count or grasp.

"All those rumours about him being here and there," Pirm said. He let out a loud laugh and tucked part of his shirt back into his pants. "If any of those rumours about his one-man world-class road show was true, why would he have ended up back at the drama department of Sint Ansfried? Deputy head or whatever the position's called?"

Pirm laughed again. Again his shirt came untucked. I looked over and saw Lena winding her way between the tables. She pointed to the coat rack. I waved that I understood and raised a finger to say I'd be a second. When I looked back at Pirm I began to feel a viselike grip on my head, as if all the noise in the room were being directed at me. Pirm kept going, oblivious as before.

"The great Dirk Noosen, teaching high school where we used to be students, living in his parents' old house. Funny how the wheel turns." He smirked and adjusted his hair in the mirror behind the bar.

I looked towards the door where Lena was holding our coats.

"It was . . . good to see you, Pirm."

"Yes," he said. "You too."

He let out something between a cackle and burp. "You know," he said, "you could send an autographed album to my office!"

The rest of that night, all I heard were echoes of Pirm's words. I thought of the letter Dirk had sent to my dorm, the program for *Elsinoreville*. Was it recent, or from years before? That night at the Easy, when Dirk evaded Lena's questions about university. Had he already dropped out by then? The plans for *Gargantua*. Could they have been a clue? And what about the address in Ithaca? Was Dirk living there or did he just drop by when he had nowhere else to go? Is that why he had come to Maastricht? As a drifter? I felt sick. What had I missed? What had he been trying to tell me? How, as Pirm said, was it possible I didn't know?

Of all the nights I wished I could have listened to my white noise tapes or swallowed one of the sedatives I'd run out of, it would have been that one. Lena, who'd had plenty to drink, dozed off. But when I tried to join her I couldn't fall asleep. My body was in turmoil. As I lay in bed and the minutes turned into what felt like hours, my ears became jammed with clusters of notes, as if some fist was pushing them into the sides of my head. No matter how woozy I became I couldn't drift away. Any time I nodded off I was immediately snapped back to wakefulness, eyes wide open, with what felt like a sharp object trying to pierce my eardrums. I tried to keep still, stop thinking, tear the sounds apart and reorganize them into some sort of sense. But they forcefully resisted, breaking themselves into an illegible, inscrutable, irresolvable confusion.

From then on my condition deteriorated steeply. Light-headedness, loss of balance, and double vision, all symptoms I'd read about, were my new, unwelcome lodgers. I went on playing the dates Taub had booked, but I was slipping. It's true that during most performances there are incorrect notes, botched entrances, but usually there's such a storm of sound coming from the stage that it is impossible for any except the most learned audience member to detect a mistake. But your peers take note, and they like to be cruel. They won't tell, but they'll show. A violist muttering to her stand partner during a rest. A flash of disgust on a conductor's face.

I had no choice but to keep it from Lena. She would only have wanted to help, and I would have wanted to show that her help was working. But how could she have helped? And how could I have shown her?

I practised harder, almost furiously. If I couldn't work through a piece at normal tempo, I'd play it at a faster and faster speed, as if to punish it. I'd wake up earlier than Lena, shut myself in the soundproofed practice room, and hammer away at the keys, almost like I wanted to break them. Make a mistake, start again. Begin with the quarter notes at 152 on the metronome and finish at 208. Once that was done, I'd break the composition into right hand and left hand. A time would come when I wouldn't know if they were corresponding correctly and I needed to make sure each hand could find its own way through the piece. Faster and faster, again and again.

Lena, who could only see things from the outside, mistook desperation for ambition and took comfort in it. For her, I was back to normal.

After I put a piece through my wringer, I'd do a "simulation." Always in the afternoon, when I was comparatively at my best. I'd leave the room. Shower. Get dressed in stage costume: button-down shirt, silk tie, jacket, dark pants, belt, shoes. Shine the shoes if necessary. I'd turn off all the lights in the apartment except the halogen lamp over the keyboard. Then I'd set up a digital recorder under the lid of the Bechstein and press Record.

Standing at the door to the practice room, I'd take a deep breath. I could not dispel the sounds. They were off tune, out of rhythm, but their grip was permanent. What I could do was make the room itself disappear. Replace the carpet beneath my shoes with hardwood boards, the darkness with an expectant audience, the threshold to the practice room with the edge of the stage. I could see, in my mind's eye, the soloist precede me. It was my turn. I'd walk up to the piano, pull the bench away from the keyboard, pinch my pants at the knee, and sit. Reach to the side of the bench to adjust the height. Extend my arms and free the wrists from the shirt cuffs.

In that moment of expectation, when I should have been hearing the first bars recur, I would hear everything else. Sometimes I'd try to corral the noise, but more often I'd try to pierce through it and get to the depths of my mind. To catch a wisp of the wind shaking branches, skimming my sides, slicing through the long grass at the edge of the dykes, rippling the surface of the canal. Stand up, Jan. Hands off the handlebars. Keep your balance.

When I finished playing the piece and returned to the practice room, the loaned Bechstein, the early-evening darkness, I would be sweating, frazzled, exhausted. My eyes would be irritated. My ears would ache as if they'd been jammed against a blaring speaker. But as I pressed the Playback button on the digital recorder, I would feel a skipped beat of hope. I would listen with trepidation to the first notes, bars, lines, pages. And for one page, or two, it would be good. So good. Better than I imagined. But then came the mistakes. At first singly, then in runs. A shambles. I'd need to start again.

Fall came. Panic was cutting into me. My heart was never at rest. Every day I woke up with the fear that Lena knew, or would know soon enough. I started getting out of bed before her, isolating myself in the bathroom or kitchen while she got ready for work. I fixated on my next appointment with Weetman. Considered calling Taub, though I didn't know what I'd say. Then one afternoon, with Lena at work, a couple of months after running into Pirm, I did something I promised myself I would not do.

I was practising Ernest Chausson's Poème for violin, with piano accompaniment, for a performance two weeks away in Antwerp. I knew the piece. Had played it dozens of times. Had a well-constructed interpretation to do with Chausson's family relation to Haussmann and the Poème as soundtrack to the new, clean enchantments of bourgeois Paris. But I could barely make it through the first section without making a hash of some line or run.

I went to the living room, turned on the computer, and waited for the screen to light up. I typed Lena's password. The desktop loaded. Small icons scattered over an old picture of Lena and me in Italy. I looked for the internet browser and double-clicked. When the search page opened I entered "Dirk Noosen."

The immediate results were pages about acting and plays, theatre reviews and profiles written by theatre people. Most were old, like the alumni newsletter at the college he'd attended, which listed his name in the pieces, but didn't follow it with the year of graduation.

I entered a new search, "Dirk Noosen Sint Ansfried." That did it. The school's website was top of the list, and I clicked on it. The home page was a picture of the side

door to the school, the one everyone used. To the left of
the picture was a list. Categories. I clicked on "Staff."
There were about thirty names, ordered alphabetically. I
scrolled down. There it was. "Dirk Noosen, Vice-Principal
and Head, Drama Department." I clicked on his name, but
there was no link.

I walked back to the practice room. The piano still
radiated Chausson's spooky notes. I dropped the fall over
the keyboard and slid past the piano to the storage closet
on the other side of the room.

On the top shelf of the closet were my records, which I
hadn't played for years, an old suitcase, a folder of receipts
for who knows what, datebooks, business files, contracts
and faxes, certificates and memorabilia. At the back, behind
some manila envelopes, was the old shoebox. I pulled it out,
laid it on the floor, and sat next to it. I grabbed a handful of
letters and cards, sifted through the most recent. Lapland,
Thailand, other lands. There was one with a picture of a
sand dune. The message written on the back was, "The
hourglass of time." I remembered finding this one after
I had come home from the supermarket. "The hourglass
of time." I turned the card over and looked at the image.
Then I picked out another card, read the message, looked
at the image. Then another, and another. The words meant
nothing. None of the messages meant anything. It was the
cards themselves that were the point. I thought we had
been separated by three oceans and fourteen time zones
when he wrote these. For the last few of them, and maybe

more, he was less than a half-day's car ride away. *I* was the one who had gone off. He was always there.

I thought I had been waiting for him. But he had been waiting for me.

That night I came as close as ever to telling Lena. It was not only that I was chasing a fading light, or that panic was building. Or that any day now she would begin to ask questions. It was the distance that was building between us. With every new setback it was like she was drifting farther from me. Sometimes I saw us as two people rooted to their positions in a field. Neither of us was moving, but through a trick of the lens, the space between us was widening. I was scared, I felt alone, and it often brought me to the edge of tears.

As we were clearing dinner, I told Lena I was thinking of cancelling the Antwerp trip.

She was confused. Of course she would be.

"But you've been working so hard these past months," she said. "Harder than I can remember."

"The world can live without another rendition of Chausson," I said, "and certainly doesn't need to hear Chausson played by me."

I didn't expect her response. Not just exasperation but disbelief.

"I've heard this from you before, Jan, and I don't like it. It's not just you onstage. I work to put you out there. So that's me you're dismissing when you say that."

I understood what she was trying to do. It's what she always did. It's what I had needed her to do. It should have been the end of the discussion, but I felt the pressure of words forming in my head. It wasn't that I didn't *want* to perform, I wanted to say, it was that I was afraid I *couldn't*.

"I . . . I don't know what's wrong with me," I said.

Lena shifted closer. A softer tone. "It's okay, Jan, love. Just tell me."

"I've been seeing Weetman every so often," I said. "I've booked another appointment with him."

"And?"

And? I felt like saying. And what do you think? I've been seeing a world-class neurologist for over two years, done what's felt like hundreds of tests, and everything's getting worse. "And that's it," I said.

"That's it?"

"Yes."

She leaned towards me, looked into my eyes. "You felt better after the first time you saw him," she said. "Right?"

Was she testing me? Was she distrusting me? I forced myself to look back at her, but could only face her for a second.

"Yes," I said, "I did. I'm sure he'll give me something. It'll pass."

"So take tomorrow off," she suggested, not knowing I'd already taken today off, and spent it reading old letters from a hidden shoebox. "I'll stay home too," she said. "We'll pull a sickie together."

"Maybe," I said, hoping she wouldn't, not wanting her to see the state I was in. "Maybe I just need a good rest."

"And if you really want to, love, you can cancel Antwerp."

The next morning I urged Lena to go to work. I was feeling better, I said.

"You're kidding, right?" she said. "After last night . . ."

"It was just passing," I said. "A spell. When you told me I could call off Antwerp, it lifted a weight."

She looked at me as if there was more to say.

"Just knowing I was in control," I said, "and knowing you were behind me, that's all I needed."

She kissed me. "You're sure?" she asked. "Sickie's still on the table."

"I'm sure. I'm not perfect, but better."

"Okay," she said, still suspicious but now in a playful way. "We can talk about the concert on the weekend if it's still a problem. Or do you want me to book myself a ticket right now to come? I'm sure I can take the time."

"Nah," I said. "It's just a few days."

The days passed. I stayed out of the practice room. It was unprofessional, but what choice did I have? Practising had become as useless as every other remedy.

Antwerp turned out to be the beginning of my final run. A horrible performance on my part, and I didn't need the others onstage to tell me. When I got back to Maastricht I called Taub and told him I was unwell. I needed time off. No dates, period. He didn't ask for details. I don't know what he thought. Maybe that I was burned out, or that there was a personal matter. We agreed I would meet my commitments for the remainder of the season, and while I had the odd booking in some summer festival, Taub would look to his stable of performers to fill the slots. He was probably pleased for the opportunity to show new talent.

"One last thing," I said. "Keep this hiatus to yourself, please. At least, as much as you can."

"Of course, Jan, of course," he said. "We've had a long run. You can trust my discretion."

After Antwerp, I had four months of performing till the summer break. I went back to practising, but with little discipline or zeal. I regressed to my conservatory habits of late nights, then my Sint Ansfried tendency of noodling with the keyboard, as if the instrument were someone I was trying to impress with half-baked skills. Soon I stopped practising altogether and, when I had to perform, did so entirely from memory.

Giving up did not make me healthier. It made me sicker. One morning, after Lena left for work, I stumbled down half a flight of stairs getting the mail. Shortly after, I was kept awake for forty-eight full hours by fevers and chills. Lena took a day off work and called our physician's office; my regular man was off and the resident who took the call, unfamiliar with my file, prescribed codeine and rest and explained to Lena it was probably a migraine.

"Have you seen Weetman yet?" she asked me. In fact I had been there right after I fell, when Weetman oversaw an ENG and ECOG to test my balance, but all I said to Lena was, "Soon, I'm seeing him soon."

She may not have believed me, I didn't know anymore, but it smoothed the edge of her exasperation, and maybe even anger, and I didn't say anything.

When I faced the mirror after I woke up in the morning, I saw a person staring back who looked one hundred years old. Thunderclaps of pain beat at my ears nonstop, sending me reeling, and on some days it was like the eardrums themselves were being battered. I waited for what Weetman would find next. Seizures. A tumour. Some kind of multiple system disease. At the same time I prepared for what I considered my last concerts.

By that time I was taking the letters out of the closet every day, and looking Dirk up on the computer too. As my prospects of recovery disintegrated with each fresh attack, my mind started charting the course home. The double-lined vapour trails of passing airplanes criss-crossing the darkening sky, the dip at the end of the Grafstraat, the house across the road, waiting, warm, familiar. A mess in the kitchen. An album playing in the bedroom. The light shining up the wall, my head on Dirk's chest, rising and falling.

With this vision taking greater and greater precedence in my head, everything external, the so-called real world, began to fade. Taub. The days spent at the Bechstein. Even Lena, who never took a step back but kept drifting and drifting.

Then came the beginning of this summer. Lena took Fridays off. We tried new restaurants around town, usually with other couples, in atmospheres boisterous enough that I could retreat into my shell without attracting notice or giving offence. I mustered all I had left to stay consistent with Lena, I loved her so much, I didn't want her to see how I had turned. But to myself, I counted the weeks till she would head north to her mother. In years past I would have taken the time to be with Lena, but this year I would stay behind. I told her I wanted to work myself into the new season. Plus I had an appointment with Weetman and didn't want to go back and forth to keep it. Lena tried to convince me to come. At least come for a week, she said. The weekends. One weekend. Just one. For the first time I saw her desperate. It hurt me. But I wouldn't bend, and, consoling herself that this is what it could be like, the musician married to his routine, she gave in.

The afternoon before she left for the north, as I helped her pack, Lena tried one last time to tempt me. She started with excitement. Come! You'll love it! Then she moved to guilt. Aren't you worried I'll be lonely? And she ended with disappointment. I was being a wet blanket. It would be good for me, she said.

A part of me resented that Lena couldn't change my mind. But she couldn't. I watched her get into the taxi the next morning.

❖

The next week, my last appointment at Weetman's office. After several years as his patient, deliberately avoiding the question, I decided to ask him this time whether I had a hope of getting back to normalcy, or at least functionality. For once, I would force him into giving me an honest prognosis. I pictured the scene: sitting on the tissue-covered examination table, waiting for him; the doorknob turning, Weetman entering with chart in hand. I anticipated his words, his manner of delivery, and an array of my own reactions.

On the day, I began with my usual recap. "Lately, when it's bad onstage, I've tried to stay still," I said as Weetman stood on the other side of the small room, arms folded across his chest. "I sometimes think that if I stop moving, the wreckage will flow away and the music will take over." I leaned forward and raised my shoulders towards my ears, imitating the pose. "But it doesn't," I said. "It just gets worse."

As I spoke, I wondered if Weetman noticed how calm I was. How objective my description. If so, he didn't say. In fact, he didn't say anything at all, didn't even tilt his head or clear his throat. I mentioned Lena was away, at her mother's. Maybe that had made it harder to sleep, I said. I'd taken the latest pills he'd prescribed, but I hadn't noticed an effect.

Normally, Weetman would take notes, ask me to repeat myself, probe me for more information. Then he'd file the notes and open a chart or journal to talk about the results of the latest tests or a new procedure that sounded promising. Maybe something experimental he'd heard about from a colleague or at a conference.

Eventually I ran out of things to say. Except for scraps of scales and the noise of a distant construction site, there was quiet.

Finally Weetman spoke. "I'm sorry, Jan," he said.

"Jan," he said. Not "Mister de Vries," which was what he'd always called me.

"We've been reviewing your case," he said, then started on about "a full regimen," having "tried the entire spectrum," "alternative therapy," "off-label use of prescriptions." Prior physicians, past diagnoses, new ones. He was, I realized, recapping the course we'd taken. He said other things, too, but I was looking at his hands. They were empty, and had been empty since he came into the room. No charts or journals, no tests results. As he went on, I started to feel a bubbling excitement. Almost ecstasy. I didn't try to understand or analyze. The more he talked, the more the excitement built.

"There's nothing left to do," he said.

I nodded.

"Nothing," he repeated.

I let the word hang. I had waited years for it, had feared it. But now that I had his expert opinion it hardly brushed against me. It was light as air. *Nothing.*

"You must try to move on, Jan," he said. Again with "Jan."

I smiled. He might have taken it for deflection, a way to cover the helplessness that he imagined I was feeling. Drowning in.

"Thank you," I said.

Weetman nodded. "Take as much time here as you need."

I left the office in a bubble, words and thoughts bouncing almost playfully around me. As I stepped into the street I saw, out of the corner of my eye, a van heading right at me. A loud honk rang through the quiet street. The van passed within inches. A current of wind lifted my jacket and I could feel the cold rush beneath my shirt. I would have to tell Lena about that, I thought to myself. But then, I wouldn't.

Next was the call from Taub. There was an opening. It was last minute. In Aachen, he said. Fauré's "Elegy." The soloist was a young cellist. American. Would I take it?

Today, this morning, I got up early. Before the sun. For the first time in ages, I wasn't tired. After an instant coffee, I showered, got dressed, grabbed the overstuffed black leather bag, and walked out of the apartment. My car was parked down the street. I opened the passenger side to slip in the bag, walked around the hood, and got behind the wheel.

The quiet streets of Maastricht joined into the autoroute. The sun passed from ahead of me, to above, to behind, in my rear-view mirror. The slopes of the south levelled into the fields of the east.

# PERFORMANCE

I n my mind I am on the saddle of my old bicycle and
  the sun is just starting its slow dip in the west. The
air is warm, as if the world is hanging an arm around my
shoulder and pressing me up to its heart. I see the steeple
of Sint Jan getting close, and soon I leave the fields behind
and break into the city. Den Bosch. I pedal past the train
station and cathedral, glide along the main road, and take
a right. A narrow street. Cars parked on both sides. I lean
forward in my saddle, reach an arm out wide, spread my
fingers to catch the wind.

   Next thing I know I'm rolling the car to the dip at the
bottom of the Grafstraat. I angle the steering wheel left
and park across the street from his house.

It's been twenty minutes since I saw Dirk drive down the
road and into the alley. Dirk, who never had a driver's
licence, who could barely drive his bicycle without posing
a danger to himself and others, in the driver's seat of a
functioning automobile. He drove slowly down the street,
flashed his high beams at the top of the alley in case of
an oncoming vehicle, and parked in the small space at
the back gate.

Now he's in the kitchen. The light is on and I see him through the bay window. I can't tell exactly what he's doing, but nothing about his motions say productivity.

I clear a small circle in the condensation on the windshield. Sitting, watching, waiting like this makes me feel like I'm backstage, in the wings. The condensation is the curtains. The end-of-day sky is the dimming of the house lights. The sulphur street lights, springing fitfully to life, are ushers rushing people to their seats, and when they begin to emit their steady yellow halos, they become the stage lights. The tree branches trembling under the evening wind is the opening applause. *Kshi-kshi-kshi.*

What, beyond the applause, do I hear?

Most prominent is Debussy's *En Blanc et Noir*. I hear, on repeat, a passage from the opening movement, when the two pianos begin to go back and forth; jabbing and undercutting, hiding and pouncing. Underlying it is the drip-drip-drip melody of a *Gnossienne*, played on a keyboard that's out of tune. The individual notes turn into the high-pitched ding of the audiologist's machine, into voices asking me questions. *Are you? Will you? What is?* Fading in and out is "Waterloo Sunset" by the Kinks, which was playing at the Easy when Dirk, Lena, and I were there, except in the present version the guitar sounds like a low moan.

I adjust the rear-view mirror, catching the edge of my midnight-blue Nehru suit, done to the top button. The inky twill looks crisp. Good as new.

On the passenger seat is my black overnight bag. Top not fully zipped, but all the old photos, letters, and postcards securely inside. Dirk in a safety vest, in a tricorne. Dirk and me on the top bunk, leaning back on the hood of the convertible. "Ten francs folded five times equals two francs, it seems." "I hate you, I love you, You are okay." And the later notes, Sunrise in Lapland, "I hope you have an excellent year." Some of my favourite possessions are in here, too. A 1955 recording of the Goldberg Variations autographed by Glenn Gould. Gold cufflinks I found in the Galleria in Milan and wore during a command performance for the College of Cardinals. The cork-handled conductor's baton given to me by Pinchas Zukerman after a four-day program with the National Arts Centre Orchestra in Ottawa. A score signed by Osmo Vänskä from a show he and I did together at the Royal Festival Hall in London. Lastly, there was what Dirk would call "the sentimental shit." The stub of a plane ticket to Los Angeles, from my first trip to America. A photograph of myself standing outside the Apollo Theater in Harlem, which I first learned about from the many "Live at the Apollo" albums Dirk owned. And, rolled up and protruding from the top of the bag, the poster Dirk gave me the summer before we turned sixteen, "The Great Janini: Wonder Show of the Universe," where a man with slicked hair ponders a crystal ball that pours out smoke in sexually suggestive patterns. For years it hung from the back of my bedroom door; my parents never noticed it. If they had, they would have made me take it down. Even though the poster is tightly rolled, I can clearly make out the magician's dark, mesmerized and mesmerizing eyes. Beacons under their heavy brows. Next to the Great Janini is the return gift; the Marie Antoinette geisha advertising "The Placenta," carefully wrapped in a cardboard tube.

I take a deep breath and reach for the handles of the bag.

As I cross the street, I feel pressure building in my head, the sounds I'd heard before, becoming louder, less distinct from one another. I count off the endings I'd made up while waiting for the phone to ring on Christmas morning; or in my dorm room, afterwards; or as I took the train from the airport to my hotel in Osaka.

Onto the curb and up the brick steps. Relax, I tell myself. The hard work is done, the worst is over.

The glass door to the vestibule opens with ease and closes behind me. In the corner, a red parka hangs from a coat stand. A pyramid of chopped wood is stacked beside it, and two pairs of boots lean against one another on the sisal mat, under which Dirk sometimes hid a key.

I push the doorbell. The two-tone chime bounces around the house and reverberates in my head.

Feet slide from hardwood to tile. The peephole goes dark, then light. The lock scrapes open and the doorknob turns. A dark grey button-down shirt, blue jeans rolled above the ankles. Bare feet. In a swift once-over I notice a belly, some weight added to the face, and lines crossing his forehead. But he still looks the same to me.

"Yes?" he says, fingers gripping the side of the door.

"It's Jan," I say. "Jan de Vries."

Dirk lets go of the door and drops his arm. He looks me up and down. A crack of a smile appears, showing the edge of his teeth. "Jan de Vries."

For a moment we are both silent, looking at each other. The first thing I see, in the light coming from the kitchen, is that his wavy hair is gone. It's buzzed short and mostly grey.

"I thought I'd drop by," I say. "I mean, I heard you were back, a while ago actually, and I've been meaning to stop by."

"Are you living here now, in the area?" he asks.

"No," I say, holding up my overnight bag by way of explanation. "I'm still on the road."

"Right, right. Of course. A musician's life."

A gust of wind buffets the vestibule, opening the glass outer door and brushing leaves around my feet. Dirk steps back from the doorway and motions that I should come in.

"Please," he says.

"Thank you," I say.

I step into the tiled entranceway and peered into the kitchen. New countertop on the island, a different shade of paint on the walls, but the plates are still stacked on open shelves, the knives paraded on the magnetic strip below them, and the old white melamine table is still in the bay window. Several drawers are open or half-open. A recycling box overflows with juice and egg cartons and beer cans. Two pots sit on the stove, one of them expelling steam. There's an open wine bottle on the counter.

"I'm not disturbing?" I ask.

Dirk turns around. "No," he says.

I hesitate, to show courtesy. The wind, which has died down, is still whistling in my ear.

"Have you had anything to eat?" Dirk asks.

"No, I haven't."

"Well," he says, gesturing to the little white table. "Why don't you join me."

I step past the doorway and leave my overnight bag in the entrance. Dirk closes the door behind me and manoeuvres into the kitchen, where he slides his feet into a pair of worn slippers. I take a seat at one of the wicker chairs around the table. A spring coat and thin purple scarf hang off the back of a chair opposite. Magazines and books are scattered on the tabletop. I undo the top and bottom buttons of my jacket. A bit of a refrain, something from late Bill Withers, which Dirk had once affectionately called "the cheesy shit," drifts in and out of my ears.

Dirk's voice interrupts. He's holding a bottle of wine. I nod and he pulls a wineglass from the open shelves, where they're herded. When he finishes pouring he passes me my glass and for a moment, almost absent-mindedly, raises his.

"The oven," he says and turns around. He reaches down the counter for a yellow plastic bag and pulls out two cuts of plastic-wrapped meat on a styrofoam tray. He slices the plastic with a knife, then lets the meat slide through the opening onto a baking dish. When the second piece slips out he wraps a tea towel around his hand, opens the oven, and slides the dish onto the centre rack. He fills two soup bowls, spilling a little on the counter, and comes to the table with them.

"What is this?" I ask.

"It's cauliflower soup. Reheated," he says.

Dirk tests a half-spoonful then looks out the bay window to the park. Tree branches shudder under a passing breeze. The thought of the wind sends a looping melody through my ear.

"It was Pirm," I say, "who told me you were back."

Dirk takes a sip from the bowl and half turns to face me. "I see Pirm every so often," he says. "He's on various admissions panels."

He reaches behind him, to the island, and grabs a roll of paper towel. He tears a piece for himself and one for me, then immediately crumples his piece and places it in his lap. I fold mine and tuck it under the bowl.

"That was maybe six months ago that I ran into him," I say. "After which I looked you up on the computer. It took me a while, I'm not much for computers, but eventually I found the Sint Ansfried website."

Dirk brushes the side of his mouth with the balled-up paper towel.

"The school looks the same," I say.

"Yes," he says. "They probably need to update the website."

His bowl is empty. His spoon is turned upside down.

I take a few quick spoonfuls to catch up.

"Really good," I say. "Thank you."

Dirk nods at the compliment, then stands to clear the plates. I make to stand too, but he motions for me to sit. As he sets up the next course, nudging plates and cutlery along the counter, I am visited by sounds from the drive up. Motor, steering rack, suspension. The rearing of changing gears. Tires passing over gravel, asphalt, the plastic reflectors embedded in lane dividers. I take two long sips of wine and slide off my jacket, draping it over the back of my chair.

The steaks are on the table. I lift the wine bottle and ask if I can refill my glass. Dirk blinks, which I guess does not mean no. I tip the bottle until the glass is two-thirds full.

"Pretty good dinner for a pit stop," I say.

He nods, then grins. A glint of the chip. Then he looks away, to the windows, examining the trims, mullions, panes, sills. Tiny tremors pass through his chin as he chews.

As we finish dinner I refill both glasses with wine. Dirk takes the bottle to the recycling bin and starts transferring dinner plates to the island. "Nice little mess we've made," he says.

I stand up with him and bring the glasses and cutlery to the sink. "At least let me help with the dishes," I say.

Dirk shakes his head. "I'm fine."

He runs the tap and fills the sink with sudsy water. He's asked a question.

"Pardon me?" I say.

"I said, did you drive?"

"Yes."

He grabs a cloth from a cupboard knob, leaving the tap on. The sound of running water is soothing. He begins to dry the glasses. "Is that your car in the dead end?" he asks.

"Yes, it is."

Dirk nods, then speaks loudly over the running water. "They ticket, you know."

"Oh," I say. "Didn't you used to be able to stay overnight?"

Dirk pauses. "I don't remember. In any case, it's been this way for a while. And they're vigilant about it."

I look at the bay windows, as if checking for the ticketing police, and see steam has condensed on the lower part of the glass. The food, wine, oven, hot water filling the sink. All starting to hit me, and I begin to feel nauseous. Dirk, still occupied at the sink, has his back turned, so I drift towards the quieter living room.

In semi-darkness I make out the couch, the patterned fabric on the wingback chair, and the open mouth of the fireplace with the wicker basket next to it. The tall curtains that cover the floor-to-ceiling windows overlooking the park are half-open. I pull them back the rest of the way, gently, but still unsettle the dust in their folds. A beam of park lamplight lights up the unfurling ringlets of dust and lands on the first steps to the second floor.

Framed photos are arrayed on the mantel. I pick them up, one at a time. There's Dirk, Wim, and Cornelia. Dirk is in his regular, stooped posture, but Cornelia's hair has gone white and Wim's face has hollowed out. There's a soft-lens portrait of Granny, and one of Dirk's brother, sitting on a couch with a child on his knee. There is a couple who seem older than Dirk but younger than his parents, maybe an older cousin or friends of Dirk's. There is also an unfamiliar woman who appears on her own, in two pictures.

The throb of noises, having calmed somewhat during the tail end of dinner, have begun to recollect themselves. I adjust the photos on the mantel and try to focus my mind on something else, an old technique. I notice the room, at first soothingly cool, is actually cold. The back of my throat is beginning to itch. I touch one of the radiators behind the curtains. Off.

I hear Dirk calling from the kitchen, saying something like "I'll be a minute." I am about to head back for my jacket when I see a throw hanging from the back of the armchair. I wrap it around my shoulders and start to pace the living room. That woman in the two photographs, I think to myself. Is she familiar? But I stop myself from going further. Why should I know everyone who has passed through Dirk's life in all this time?

Dirk still hasn't appeared, so I call to the kitchen. "Do you have something else to drink?" *Digestif quoi?* as Dirk would have put it.

He calls back. "Let me take a look."

Cupboards open, then drawers. After a few moments Dirk passes from the kitchen into the dining room. As he fishes around I peer at the small picture that's replaced the Scholte. A pastel seascape, the type of thing a tourist would buy. Maybe there's something to the painting I can't see. A sea monster, lurking amid the waves. Dirk hunches into the living room holding a bottle of Scotch and two crystal glasses by the insides of their rims. He places everything on a side table between armchair and couch, uncorks the bottle, and pours two fingers into each glass.

"Cheers," I say, lifting my glass. "To a special occasion."

I sit on the couch. Dirk sits in the armchair.

I take a slug from the glass. A taste of fire wakes up my throat and warms my chest, but with it comes a sharp sting to the side of my head. I adjust the cushion behind me, take another sip, and wait for the sting. It's delayed this time, but it comes. It's stronger.

"You know," I say, "it's been thirty years since you popped down to Maastricht to visit me."

Dirk scratches the side of his nose. "Thirty?"

"Thirty and a bit," I say.

He nods slowly. Like he had at the front door and dinner table. He takes another short sip of his drink and grins as the heat of the Scotch goes down. "Where does the time go, eh, Jan?"

"You know, every time I run into Sint Ansfried people, they always ask about you."

"And?"

"And they tell me what they'd heard."

"What they'd heard?"

"Yes, about how you'd been spotted here, there, everywhere. It's how I kept up with the news."

He scratches his nose, looks down at his glass.

"I heard, for instance, you were in Paris and teaching at the Sorbonne."

"I did teach here and there," he says.

"And in America?"

"I was, for a while."

"Someone told me you were on Broadway."

"I was, in various capacities. On Broadway and off-Broadway. Do you know off-Broadway?"

I shake my head.

"It's far better," he says.

I nod, waiting for more. But it doesn't come.

"So did you like America?" I ask.

"Yes," he says, "though that's not always a popular thing to say."

Dirk looks into the far upper corner of the room. I feel a jab, or maybe a prod. A scrabble of noises too tangled to identify.

"I heard other things, you know."

Dirk keeps his face turned towards the corner. "I'm sure most of it was exaggeration."

"I was told you were back," I say. "That one was true."

He clears his throat. "But enough about me, Jan." He taps the side of his glass, maybe deciding whether to pour himself, and me, another shot. I make the decision for him.

"You don't mind, do you?" I ask, not waiting for an answer.

In the long pauses between words, the noise level increases. There are skips and scratches in what I hear. Mounting pressure. As Dirk fiddles with his crystal glass I try to wrap my mind around the noises, establish a limit to the disruption, a type of fire-ditch. But it isn't working. Something is always crossing the barrier. Sparks to start a conflagration.

Dirk scratches behind his ear. I shake my head, trying to clear space. "A little while after I ran into Pirm," I begin, "I cleaned out my apartment in Maastricht and found this trove of letters and photographs from Sint Ansfried days."

Dirk rubs at his cheek. Frowns slightly.

"Actually, I brought them with me," I say. "It includes the letter you wrote while I was in Maastricht. I hadn't heard from you in such a long time, you know, and this letter came out of nowhere."

Suddenly a change in the room. It was dark before, but now it's nearly black.

"The park lamps," Dirk says. "They've clocked off."

I try to regain my bearings. The volume in my ears is steadily increasing. Dirk, now only an outline, says something to me, but I'm having trouble hearing.

"Pardon me?" I say.

He mouths the words again. I raise my hands in confusion.

He says it louder. It's a question. Sounds like the word "water."

"For the road."

A scalding heat races through my head. The confusion that had been held at bay is becoming visceral. Crippling. Feedback from speakers, crossed wires screaming at one another.

Dirk is talking to me, but his voice is tucked somewhere behind the noise. A rush of blood presses into the sides of my head. I close my eyes and jam my fists against the place where the blood is pulsing.

I try to apologize. Mumble some excuse. It's all happening too quickly. What must Dirk be thinking? Suddenly I feel his hand on my shoulder. I grip his forearm and try to stand, but as I rise I feel my knees buckle and I stumble to the ground. A cushion tumbles after me. I reach up again and knock the scotch glass off the side table.

Dirk says something else, but I don't know what it is. I fumble behind myself for the cushion, try to set it back on the couch. Dirk grips my shoulder again.

"I'm . . . I'm . . ." I say. "This . . ."

Dirk bends closer. He grabs my wrist and swings my arm across his back. Up. I lean against him now. Can just make out his words.

"You can come upstairs and lie down," he says. "The old room."

My chest begins to heave, my nose becomes stuffed. Dirk pretends not to notice. He is focused on helping me stand. Keeping my arm around his neck, holding me to his side as we walk to the staircase.

By now the sharp sounds in my head have melded into a brutal tangle, worse than ever before. As we climb the stairs together I look at Dirk, but he is staring ahead. Once or twice he stops to get a better grip on my arm, or pull my body closer to his, but he keeps his focus on the next step and the one after. I think of how he and I used to race up these steps, me trying to outrun him, him pushing past me. *Watch you don't snap a tendon, Old Man. Watch you don't fall back and break your head, Dirk. I won't be wheeling you around the parks on Sundays. Yeah? Well I won't be changing your colostomy bags.*

"Take it easy," Dirk says, looking down at the tricky turn at the top of the steps. "We're almost there."

Dirk pushes open the door to his old room, unwraps my arm from around him, and leans me against the doorframe. Once he sees I'm settled, he reaches for the light switch and adjusts the dimmer to low.

The room looks like it's used for storage now. The teetering bookcase that housed Dirk's stereo system and speakers is gone. The space where the desk used to stand is now occupied by a half-dozen, shoddily assembled cardboard boxes. Reference books and what look like plays, probably the same ones we used to read in school, are piled up along the walls. In place of the bunk bed, at the far side of the room, is a metal-framed cot, low to the ground.

"Wait here," Dirk says, touching my shoulder. He goes to the almost empty cupboard and pulls out a sheet, pillowcases, and a fleece blanket from the top shelf. He unfurls the sheet, spreads it over the mattress, and tucks in the corners. He slides the pillows into the cases and drapes the blanket over the freshly made bed.

"Goodnight," he says, and before I can register the word, or react, he leaves the room, closing the door behind him.

At first I don't move. Then I turn the lights off. Still dizzy and susceptible to falling over, I gingerly strip off my pants and dress shirt, and in semi-darkness feel for the edge of the cot. The mattress bows and the cot's springs groan. Lying down, I feel like I've been buried beneath a collapsed roof, and I can barely breathe under its weight.

Unable to fall asleep, I look through the two windows past the foot of the bed and make out what looks like a jittery night sky. One moment it's pitch-black, the next it's as if light is pulsing through. A rash of stars appears and disappears, like in some kind of game.

I close my eyes and try to start again, from the top. Like a practice session. Putting every note in its place.

The first time I saw Dirk. First time I went to his house. All our Christmases. Maastricht. After. Vivace. Allegro. Scherzo. Adagio.

Lights like bright stars shine down on me. Keys like firecrackers sparkle beneath my fingers.

I see Weetman. At first I'm ignoring him. But now his words are coming back to me. *We've been reviewing your case, Jan,* he says, not saying who "we" are. *And I have to say . . .* He is wearing a lab coat with a Bic and Hi-Liter in the pocket, and he's turning up the palms of his small hands, looking me in the eye. Listing, once again, all the tests and all the negative results. *We can't find the cause, Jan.*

He keeps talking, but his words are breaking up, floating upward on the strings of Ralph Vaughan Williams' Fantasia. A wave of violins washes over the familiar landscape. Straight roads. Morning frost on the canals.

I've got to get up, I think to myself, I've got to get back. I'm about to push my legs over the side of the bed, to leave the house and head down to the car, when I see a blade of light cutting across the carpeted floor and remember I'm in Dirk's bedroom.

For the first time in a long time, there is a kind of quiet. I know this because I can hear, within this quiet, the sound of long, regular breaths.

I sit up on the edge of the cot and rub my eyes. I can still hear the breathing. The fleece blanket slides off my chest. Goosebumps rise on my arms.

He's sitting on top of one of the packing boxes.

"Dirk?"

I detect a slight movement. My heart begins to pound. I lean forward. My breathing is shallow.

"Dirk?"

He clears his throat.

I wait. Will he slowly rise and embrace me? Will he launch himself at me? Will he bring me into his chest and hold me tight, or will he force me to my knees, circle behind, and lean on the spot between my shoulder blades?

I tense my shoulders, ready.

Dirk rests a hand on his knee and looks me over, weighing me up. The blade of hall light illuminates the side of his head. Hair, ear, cheek.

"Why now?" he says.

"Because I need you," I say, without hesitation.

No answer.

"Because I needed to come home."

A smile out of the shadows. Or maybe a smirk. "Home?"

"Yes. Of all the places in the world, this is my home. Will always be my home. Just like it's yours."

The smirk shrinks away. Maybe it hadn't been there in the first place, maybe I misread his face.

"Remember our wrestling matches in this room?" I say. "One hand behind your back? Two? How, every time, I lost?"

More silence and stillness from where Dirk sits.

"Remember what came after them, when the lights went out, after the music stopped playing?"

Dirk shifts. His eye flashes in the light, then disappears, along with the rest of his face. I shiver as a bead of sweat drips down my side.

"Dirk, I came back because there's something wrong with me. Nobody can fix it. Nobody can even figure out what it is, or *if* it is, but I'm tired of fighting it, fighting myself." I wipe my hand across my forehead. "What I wanted to say is . . . I need you. And you need me, too. I never understood that."

"Understood?"

"Pirm told me about your breakdown. About dropping out."

A thunderclap runs from ear to ear, like weather starting up again. My arms start to shake. I don't have much time. I begin to blurt out the words. What I'd meant to say from the moment I stepped in the front door.

"Pirm told me about what you suffered and it finally made sense. Why it ended the way it did. You see, we didn't drift away, we didn't outgrow each other, like friends. You cut me out, overnight, because we weren't just friends. We were much more than that, only I didn't realize it at the time. You knew it, but I didn't."

I feel my eyes beginning to well. I can only just hear the words pouring out of me.

"You loved me, Dirk. And I didn't realize I loved you too. And you suffered for that. That's why you didn't tell me about the breakdown, about leaving school. That's why you didn't meet me in Japan. It was because you thought I didn't love you, but I did. I still do."

The moment of auditory reprieve is over. A razorlike ringing enters with full force. It cuts into me, through me, tears me apart. I fall forward from the bed and reach towards him.

"Please don't be so cold, Dirk. *Please.*"

Can't he see that he could solve everything just by reaching out, touching my arm, letting my head rest against his chest?

Finally he speaks. "Jan," he says. His voice is low, cool, and pierces the noises in my head. "All this was thirty years ago. You can't just show up at my front door as if time hasn't passed. As if this was still your home and everything's the same."

I hear his words, but it takes a further moment to understand their meaning. And when I do I feel a wave of nausea pass over me. I can't see straight. Can't see his face. Tears start streaming. I feel sick all over again, like I did the night I saw Pirm.

But Dirk doesn't stop. His words are like barbed wire, wrapping tighter and tighter around my head.

"All these memories are from a lifetime ago," he says. "You're no closer to me than any of my colleagues. I'm sorry to say this but I'm a stranger to you. And you're a stranger to me."

"But," I manage to blurt out, "what about what we did in this room?"

Dirk shrugs. "We were kids," he says. "That was kid stuff that we did."

I wipe my eyes. I see Dirk shake his head and stand up. I rise with him. Hammers pound at the sides of my skull.

"*Dirk* . . ."

For a second he stays still. Then he turns to the door.

"*No*, Dirk. Please don't . . ."

He reaches for the doorknob. I stand in the centre of the room, my whole body shaking. My face bubbles with heat and moisture, my eyes begin to sting, my knees start to go weak. He's left the door half-open behind him, but it isn't a sign or clue. It's nothing. He is gone.

CODA

It's black outside. The wind cuts into my bones, slicing through everything right up to the opening bars of Chopin's "Tristesse" that come from the very back of my head. The equilibrium of the mezzo-piano beginning, the climbing and descending octaves. The rumble of chords in the left hand, soothed by solitary raindrops falling in the right. But as soon as I anticipate the next line, the music begins to break apart. The rumbling left returns, this time monstrously. Crashing, pounding, pulverizing, mistake-ridden. *Wrong, wrong, wrong.* More mistakes. More noise. The reverberations multiply outside my control, turning into hammers striking at the weak parts of my skull, trying to make it crack and crumble.

My car is just on the other side of the road, but the surface is slick with early-morning frost and I need to take small steps. I'm halfway across when I remember I left the overnight bag in the entranceway. I try to turn, but slip. I reach out to stop the fall but it doesn't help. My forehead bounces off the asphalt. A cold damp seeps through my clothes and across my skin. I stay crouched on the road. It hurts too much to move. I finally stand up and hobble to the hood of the car. Leave the bag behind, I say to myself. Scream to myself. Leave it for him.

I turn out of the dead end. The streets of Den Bosch are empty and soon I'm back on the A2, in the country. In these parts there is no lighting, and when the sky is dark, as it is now, the road disappears into the land around it. Inside my head, inside my ears, the sounds have combined into one long, wild clash. I roll down the driver's side window and press on the accelerator.

For a while, longer than I expected, there is nothing out there. But eventually I see, far in the distance, a pin-prick of light.

A gust of wind rattles the hood of my car. I turn off my own headlights. It makes everything feel closer.

After a minute, the single pinprick separates into two. As they approach I can tell, by the size and distance between them, that they belong to a small truck.

I press harder on the gas. The clashes are heading towards a sublime pitch. The wind that rushes through the open window, which should be deafening, is just another line in the symphony. The truck's headlights, closer now, show me just enough of the road ahead. No turns. No rises or dips or bridges.

I push my shoulders back into the seat, lock my hands on the wheel, close my eyes.

"One, two, three . . ."

The noise is all force now. Pounding, smashing against one ear then the other. I can pick out the cymbals, the broken strings, the four-note chords deep in the left hand. Passages I played ages ago and bits I heard late last night, all mixed up in one another.

"Four, five, six . . ."

I strengthen my grip on the wheel, tense my forearms and shoulders. Chainsaws. Razor edges. Bawling kettles.

A faint glow lights the inside of my eyelids.

"Seven. Eight."

A new noise comes to clean out the others. Louder. More insistent. A ground-shaking thrum that turns into a roar.

"Nine. Ten. Eleven."

The glow becomes a light. I clench my fists to keep the car in line. I squeeze my eyelids tighter. The roar is everywhere. The lights are beginning to burn.

"Twelve."

A blast from a horn. A deafening ringing. The inside of my eyelids are burning white.

I know what comes next. A sudden jerk forward, then back. A hailstorm of glass, raining down on the roof. A scraping along the driver's side, followed by a violent hiss, and a longer, louder blast from the horn, which lasts, and lasts. But I don't hear any of it. I don't hear anything. I'm about to reach the mythical thirteen, establish the record, beat Dirk, and win.

D irk sits up in bed and rubs his eyes. He had forgotten to lower the blinds the night before and the morning sun is sharp.

He pushes the blanket off the side of the bed and puts his feet on the floor. It's cold. He pads around for his old slippers and finds one then the other; the second was hiding beneath his bed.

Standing too quickly, he has to check himself. He has the edge of a headache. The usual excuse, too much drink. He blinks a few times, regains his balance, and walks around the bed to check the window. One of the panes is foggy. A cracked seal. Must replace, he thinks. His housecoat is at the foot of the bed. He swings his arms into the sleeves.

The second-floor hallway is dark but the light from the living room glows up the stairs. The curtains are open. The park grass is an early-morning green. It's not yet in full splendour. Still waking up, like Dirk.

The front door, the vestibule door. Morning air. The paper, of course, is on the lowest step. One of these days the delivery man, or woman, or whoever, could get the paper to the middle steps, or even the higher steps. Or, even, the top step. Save Dirk's back just a little. Or he could cancel the paper. He only scans the headlines and reads the odd letter to the editor.

He throws the paper on the island and shakes the kettle. Enough water for two. Onto the stove, then. Knob to max.

Housecoat half-open, he surveys the mess. Plates on the counter. Trays in the sink. Chairs pulled from the table. He could go on, but he'd just be avoiding it. The thing he saw when opening the front door. The black leather bag on the tile. An overnighter.

From where he's standing, beside the stove, he sees something familiar sticking out the top of the bag. In fact, he thinks he knows what it is. Thinks? Is sure. The Great Janini. Got it off a shop in Den Bosch and gave it to Jan, in grade ten. Could it be the same, the original? Wouldn't that be something. There are other things in the bag besides the rolled-up poster. Dirk can make out the edges of envelopes, the corners of colour photos. Bengal tigers, he thinks. Louis Napoleon the Third.

He tests the kettle by touch. Heating, but with the momentum of a boulder rolling uphill. He shakes the useless knob.

A part of him wants to open the bag. Wanted to the moment he recognized the poster. Turn it upside down and give it a shake. The other part, unsure of Jan's intentions, waits by the stove for the water to boil. What's another five minutes after so long? Give it time. Give him time.

Patience, he says to himself. Even if patience is not his forte. *Forte*, a kind of pun.

Dirk touches the side of the kettle again. He double-knots the cord of his housecoat. He looks over the dead end of the street, and makes himself into the kind of person who patiently waits.

*I dedicate this book,*
*and all my love,*
*to ANYA.*

And I acknowledge with gratitude those who sped this story from manuscript to publication:

ANDY KIFER, the all-enduring, all-weather chain that turned blind energy into kinetic force,

AMY BLACK and KIARA KENT, the two true wheels that put this tale in touch with the world,

and my brother GREGORY, imaginary ideal reader, the wind at my back.

Thanks to all. Till next time.

## ABOUT THE AUTHOR

Eric Beck Rubin is a cultural historian who writes on architecture, literature and psychology. *School of Velocity* is his first foray into fiction, and was shortlisted for both the Frank Hegyi Award for Emerging Authors and the Kobo Emerging Writer Prize. He is currently at work on a second: a family saga spanning several generations, from pre-World War II Germany to present-day Los Angeles and Western Canada. He lives in Toronto.

# PUSHKIN PRESS

Pushkin Press was founded in 1997, and publishes novels, essays, memoirs, children's books—everything from timeless classics to the urgent and contemporary.

Our books represent exciting, high-quality writing from around the world: we publish some of the twentieth century's most widely acclaimed, brilliant authors such as Stefan Zweig, Marcel Aymé, Teffi, Antal Szerb, Gaito Gazdanov and Yasushi Inoue, as well as compelling and award-winning contemporary writers, including Andrés Neuman, Edith Pearlman, Eka Kurniawan, Ayelet Gundar-Goshen and Chigozie Obioma.

Pushkin Press publishes the world's best stories, to be read and read again. To discover more, visit www.pushkinpress.com.